IN YOUR DREAMS

I0536676

by

William Blackwell

IN YOUR DREAMS

Published by William Blackwell Publishing
Paperback ISBN: 978-1-0697318-7-6

Version: 2020.12.15

In your dreams, anything is possible. Make your dreams your reality.
—William Blackwell

All men dream: but not equally. Those who dream by night in the dusty recesses of their minds wake in the day to find that it was vanity: but the dreamers of the day are dangerous men, for they may act their dreams with open eyes, to make it possible.
—T.E. Lawrence

Every great dream begins with a dreamer. Always remember, you have within you the strength, the patience, and the passion to reach for the stars to change the world.
—Harriet Tubman

All that we see or seem is but a dream within a dream.
—Edgar Allan Poe

Prologue

Devoid of passion, absent of feelings, empty of emotions, Stella watched the opaque image appear from a black void. A nothingness. She blinked twice, observing it take shape and color. It slowly morphed into the form of a large gray man, bulbous and ballooning as he neared. It didn't arouse her curiosity much. She'd seen it dozens of times before. The first few times, the specter had given her faint hope of a better life, a love-filled union, and a consummation of souls. But the hope had always vanished before it ever turned into anything tangible. In the past, she'd tried desperately to communicate with the apparition, but had only been met with a sad and miserable silence. On three occasions, it had opened its mouth to speak, but no words had emerged, and a few seconds later, it had vanished with a pop and a fizz.

Right now, Stella, at least she believed that to be her name, knew one thing. Curiosity and desperation had been replaced by anger. She'd had enough. "Get the hell out of here," she said. "You're nothing more than a figment of a lonely imagination, here to taunt and tease me. Leave, will you?"

She closed her eyes and curled up into a little ball, hoping against all hope that when she opened them the Goodyear tire man with no discernable facial features would be gone for good.

Inside the black emptiness, the temperature rose rapidly and Stella began to perspire. A salty bead of sweat dribbled into her open mouth. She licked and swallowed it, grimacing at the taste. Hadn't her past tears tasted salty when they'd flowed so many times before? She thought so.

She wrapped her hands around her knees tighter, burying her head in her bosom and wishing she too could just vanish into hot air. So much sadness. So much disappointment. So much loneliness and despair. It was high time to end it all.

"I feel your pain," a voice said. "I feel your sadness. I feel your despair."

Its compassionate tone sent hot flashes radiating through her body.

She convulsed, jerking her hands free from her legs, and looked up. The gray image had thinned noticeably, and for a second, she thought she saw facial features. But she blinked and they were gone.

"Who are you?" she asked. "And what do you want?"

"I'm here to tell you there is hope. Hope for you. Hope for me. Don't give up being. Don't give up wanting."

Overwhelmed with a rush of loving emotions, Stella tried to stand. But the surface on which she stood was spongy like quicksand, and she felt herself sinking into it. *This time, I'm the one disappearing, just when it matters the most.*

"No," she said, now up to her neck in the black ooze. "Help me."

"I can only help you if you help yourself," the voice said, distant now.

Helpless, she watched the form shrink as it faded into the black nothingness that was her life. "No, no, please, no. Come back. Heeeeeelp me!"

As a tidal wave of negative emotions bombarded her—fear, sadness, hopelessness, and debilitating loneliness—she closed her eyes and succumbed to the inevitable state of being which she had so uncomfortably grown accustomed to.

Black nothingness.

It was as if time and space had no relevance in her life, but paradoxically it seemed like a long time later that Stella again opened her eyes. Seeing only the black void of despair, she closed them again and repeated in her mind the questions she'd so often asked herself.

Why is my life so black? What am I doing here? Is there any hope?

Where usually the same answers flowed, this time there was a slight deviation from the previous theme of helplessness and bleakness. Why? Because the voice had spoken—for the first time.

Is there a chance for me? A chance for happiness? A chance for a soul mate?

But those questions only produced troubling answers and more disturbing questions.

I've seen the same thing over and over and over again. Why the change? Why now? Why me?

Is this a dream? Is my life a dream? Am I even alive?

Yes, I must be alive. I think, therefore I am.

Stella closed her eyes again, giving pale hope to the possibility that when she opened them, all the blackness would be gone. And, although she had no recollection of it at all, she would find herself living some wonderful, productive, loving, and happy life in an ideal and pastoral setting.

But when she opened her eyes to the black void, the tears started flowing freely again, salty, sure enough, and suppressing any notion that she actually had a life, any life at all.

Chapter One

"In your dreams," Finley Holmstein said to Oliver Gimble, his friend of twenty years. "I don't know how many times you've said you met the girl of your dreams *in* your dreams. Wake up and smell the coffee, bro. These fantasies will never become reality."

Oliver knew he should've kept his mouth shut. Maybe he *should* be smelling the coffee he was drinking with Finley on his balcony on that balmy Saturday afternoon. But over the last two months, the dreams had become more prevalent, more poignant, and more repetitive. Not only that, he'd become more obsessed with them. And, knowing his friends could be tallied on four digits, he had to tell someone.

"Never say never," Oliver said. It was all he could think of to say.

"You just said it. Twice."

"You never even let me finish the story."

"You said you met the woman of your dreams *in* your dreams. What else do I need to know? You've told me the story like a million times. And it's always the same."

Oliver knew Finley was being hyperbolic. But he'd told him the story at least a dozen times. However, it hadn't always been exactly the same, although Finley seemed to miss the nuances, or had been unable or unwilling to parse them.

"But it's not the same this time," Oliver said, ignoring the smaller point in favor of the big picture. "It wasn't the same last night. She spoke. I spoke. We had a conversation. Where before there was no hope, now there is. Don't you see?"

Finley sipped his coffee and gazed at the gridlocked traffic on the Toronto city streets below. He saw it but didn't see it. He'd lived here too long. His stern gaze met Oliver's eyes and he scratched his neatly manicured black beard. "No, I don't see it. What I do see is a guy with no life who has become lost in a fantasy world. I mean look at you. You're always in this apartment of yours watching TV or reading, or whatever it is you do in your spare time. You don't go out. You don't socialize. You don't try to meet women in the real world. It's like you've given up on society and retreated into the depths of illusion... I can tell you one thing for sure."

"You've already told me a few things."

"Never mind. Let me finish. That illusion that you've set up can only lead to one thing. And that's disillusion, once you realize that it'll never become a reality." Finley ran a hand through his slicked-back hair and continued, "Wait a minute. I guess I'm wrong. It'll lead to far more than disillusion. It'll also lead to sadness and depression once you face the fact that you don't really have a life. I mean, come on, Oliver. You've stopped working out, you're eating more junk food and gaining weight. You don't seem to give two fucks about your appearance anymore, and in the real world, you've written off the opposite sex entirely. To compensate, you've created this glass menagerie which will eventually be shattered to smithereens."

Finley sighed deeply, sipped coffee, and probed Oliver with his dark brown eyes. Waiting for a response.

Oliver swallowed a gulp of coffee, washing down a lump in his throat. Maybe Finley was right. Too many broken hearts had definitely led to an aversion to women. Not that he hated them. He still loved them, supposed he always would. But, in the real world, he was too scared shitless to ever approach one and strike up a conversation. And, really, what was his life? A middle-aged man who was a customer service rep for Bell Canada, a cellphone provider. *Finley should talk*, he thought. Wait a minute. He can talk. Finley ran a successful renovation and construction company, owned a million-plus dollar home in the downtown core, and had a loving wife and two children, a girl, six, and a boy, four. He also enjoyed an expansive social life and had tried numerous times unsuccessfully to acquaint Oliver with some of his friends, male and female alike.

Recognizing all of this, Oliver said, "There is some truth to your words. But you can be pretty harsh and cynical, you know?"

Finley set his coffee mug on the glass-topped patio table and threw his arms up. "I'm your friend. Do you want your friends to sugar-coat things, or call you on your bullshit?"

"This isn't bullshit," Oliver tried weakly, knowing the defense wouldn't hold water. "It's a dream."

"You know what I mean. I know it's a dream. That's just it. You have to start living in the real world. Even Ruby's worried about you."

Before he'd adopted his Howard Hughes style of reclusiveness, Oliver had socialized with Ruby, a few years back, and found her quite companionable and insightful. He even considered her a friend. And maybe, just maybe, what he needed right now was a woman's opinion instead of a cynical, opinionated, and self-righteous man's, albeit his buddy.

Oliver backed off from the dream, realizing it was an endless black void for Finley. *Hell, maybe even for me.*

He tried a different tact. "How *is* Ruby? I haven't seen her in ages."

Finley grinned confidently. "That's where my lecture ends and the good news begins."

"Good news?"

"Yeah. The reason I stopped over is Ruby wants you to meet a friend of hers."

Oliver's heart skipped a beat. "A blind date?"

"Call it whatever you want. Carmen is a work friend of Ruby's at the legal firm. I've only met her once. Anyway, she's been through a series of bad relationships. Can't seem to pick the right guy. Kind of like you. Ruby figured you two would be a good match. You're invited to dinner at our place next Saturday to meet Carmen. If you guys hit it off, well, you can take it from there. Whaddaya say?"

Oliver, his precarious confidence not two minutes ago shredded to pieces by his best friend, felt unsure. "I... I need to think about it."

Finley stood. "I gotta run. Don't think too long about it."

"I'll... I'll let you know tomorrow. How's that?"

Finley put his hand on Oliver's shoulder. "Okay. I know I come off as harsh sometimes, bro. And you probably think I'm a cynical asshole at times. But, believe me, I'm your friend and I care about you. I do have your best interests at heart."

His confidence precipitously restored, Oliver said, "Okay, I'll come."

"Before you do, clean yourself up a bit. You're a mess. And so is your apartment."

The comment burst Oliver's precarious confidence bubble.

Chapter Two

It had been a day and night of horror movies. A movie marathon with plenty of junk food thrown in to set the ambiance. At least the ambiance that Oliver craved. He watched his usual favorites—B-grade horror flicks with plenty of gore, gratuitous female nudity, and violence. Exploitation films. Murderous slashers running amuck; zombies invading a stripper bar; a lone female hitchhiker kidnapped and tortured by inbred, wacked-out hillbillies; a devil-worshipping gang of sorority sisters. Over time, the shows blended together, forming a macabre mosaic of sex and violence. It was all a blur, really, and if you asked Oliver to name a title from the six movies he'd watched that evening, he wouldn't be able to.

He clicked the TV off and checked the time—a quarter past midnight. He brushed some chips away from his food-stained jeans, adjusted his bulk on the couch, and let the gore and sex images slowly disintegrate from his mind.

It took only a few minutes, since his thoughts had largely been occupied by two women during the horror movie marathon; Carmen, and what she might be like; but mostly the mystery woman who'd appeared in his dreams, who'd first appeared six months ago. He kept focusing on the details of last night's dream. He'd spoken to her; she'd spoken to him. There was hope.

But the big question remained. How to summon her into the real world. Was she just a dreamscape apparition? Or was she real? Well, come hell or high water, Oliver aimed to get to the bottom of it. He switched an end table lamp off and slowly rose from the junk-food-stained sofa. His arthritic knee joints squeaked and creaked in protest as he lumbered into the bathroom and began relieving himself. He caught a glance of his reflection in the mirror and for a moment froze with fear when he saw a bulbous gray man with no discernable facial features looking back at him. He caught himself, at least his prick, before dousing the linoleum floor with a golden shower and steadied himself with a hand on the mirror while he orientated the trajectory of his urine stream. The gray man morphed into Oliver's shadowy reflection and his heart slowly steadied as he finished, zipped up his fly, and flushed the toilet. He ran a hand through his greasy mullet.

Jesus. Does anyone even wear mullets anymore? Yeah, you do, clown, the little mocking voice inside his head said.

He stroked his pear-shaped cheeks and then realized with a sigh that maybe he should be washing his hands before messing with his face.

"Dumb fuck," he said to an empty apartment. He turned the taps on, grabbed a bar of soap, scrubbed his hands, and then rinsed and dried them. He considered washing his face since it'd been at least two days since he'd showered. But his laziness, disregard for personal hygiene, and fatigue overcame him. He switched the bathroom light off, wandered into his bedroom, stripped down to a T-shirt and underwear, and frowned at his formidable gut. He sighed, flopped on the bed, and returned his thoughts to the mystery woman.

I'm gonna find her again. Tonight. This time, for real. Carmen's not the one. She is. What should I call her? How about Selina? Yeah, I like that name. Selina it is. Come to me tonight, Selina, and show me how to bring you into our world. It's been so long and I've become such a fuck-up. I need your help as much as you need mine.

Before long, Oliver started snoring softly. He felt his body and mind being dragged down into that dark and little understood world of dreams and unconsciousness. Images flashed through his mind—naked breasts, blood-soaked victims, bloodthirsty murderers. But they fragmented swiftly and soon he was in the black nothingness he'd grown so habituated to.

He stirred and opened his eyes. A lucid dream. Awake in a dream. Perfect. He called for her. "Selina, come to me. I'm here to save you."

Instead of Selina, a bikini-bottomed, big breasted blonde woman armed with a blood-soaked butcher knife appeared in the dimly lit distance, screamed ear-piercingly loud, and attacked. An adrenaline-infused jolt of fear rocketed Oliver to his feet and he turned to run. But his feet began sinking in the black ooze surrounding him and he could make little headway. Soon the woman was upon him, slicing and dicing. He watched helplessly as blood squirted from gash after gash after gash.

"No, please, no," he said, holding up a hand feebly in defense.

Instantly, a finger was sliced off, then another, and another.

"Fuck you," the woman said, showering him with a sprinkling of spittle. "You condone the exploitation of women, so fuck you!" She continued slashing and Oliver started screaming bloody murder.

His screams and fear sent him toppling off his bed and into the relative safety of consciousness. His heart pounded in his chest and his obese body and face glistened with sweat.

"Holy fuck," he said, running his hands over his extremities to reassure himself that he was in one piece. He got up and sat on the edge of the bed, shivering with fear, too afraid to go to sleep, lest the murderous, semi-naked opponent of female exploitation revisit him and finish what she'd started.

It took about ten minutes before he felt his heart rate return to normal. "Why did you do that, Selina? But, no, it wasn't you, was it?"

Out of the corner of his eye, he saw a black shadow pass his bedroom window, rushed over to it, and peered out at the moonlit sky. He searched the cloudy sky, partially obscuring a half-moon. Nothing. Then five floors down to the streets below, all he saw were eerily glowing streetlights and the headlights of vehicles now making steady and fast progress through uncrowded streets. He checked the time again, 3:36 am, and was surprised at the lateness of the hour. It seemed to Oliver as if the nightmare had transpired in mere minutes as opposed to hours.

He closed the blinds and lumbered into the kitchen. He opened the fridge, grabbed a milk carton, drained six gulps, belched loudly, and then returned it to the fridge. He knew the milk would make him sleepy as soon as he could muster the courage to return to bed.

He surveyed the small galley-style kitchen. The countertops were littered with dirty dishes, the garbage can was overflowing and there was an open cardboard pizza box on the kitchen table containing one half-eaten slice of pizza that had been sitting there for so long it had probably become fossilized.

Becoming ashamed at his slovenliness, Oliver returned to the living room, frowning as soon as he realized it wasn't much better. Empty chip bags, chocolate bar wrappers, and other assorted garbage littered the floor, sofa, and two old and well-worn brown leather armchairs.

"What a goddamned slob I've become," he said, his fat cheeks reddening.

You should clean up your act then, a voice in his head responded.

"Fuck you," Oliver said, trying to get an upper hand on his inner demons. *Now I'm talking to myself. And answering myself.*

Oliver brushed away some debris from the couch, plopped his fat ass down, and studied the mess again, trying to decide if he should try to get the upper hand on cleaning his apartment, never mind the inner demons. Maybe they were right.

He knew he couldn't return to bed right away, not after the arrival of the slasher. He needed more time to get his mind back into sleep mode, and he knew he had to do something to distract from the terrible fear the nightmare had produced. But, after sitting idly for about fifteen minutes, he felt powerless to do anything about the mess. Falling back on his long-time habits, he peeled open a bag of Doritos and turned the TV on, thinking that if he watched something, anything, long enough, he'd fall asleep on the couch. Or at least become tired enough to trudge back into bed.

The first image that appeared on the screen was a bikini-bottomed, big breasted blonde woman armed with a blood-soaked butcher knife. Grinning seductively, she licked a drop of blood from the blade. Then, screaming bloody murder, she raised the weapon and charged.

Oliver jumped and a cold chill raced up his spine. *Fuck it. A nightmare. A similar movie. A fucking coincidence, nothing more.* Eventually, he settled back into the ass-worn spot on the sofa.

What a pathetic life I have.

Chapter Three

Roger Richter, Oliver's supervisor at Bell, gave Oliver that look. Oliver knew what it meant. *Get in my office. Now.*

"But what about my post?" Oliver said.

An auburn-haired woman appeared behind Roger and smiled at Oliver, a go-fuck-yourself salutation.

Roger motioned to her with an outstretched hand. "Don't worry, Frannie will take your place."

Roger turned around, walked to the end of the hall, opened his office door, and went inside, leaving the door slightly ajar.

Oliver rose and pushed his chair aside for Frannie. She stood about ten feet away and didn't budge. As Oliver walked past her, she even backed up a few feet, giving Oliver a wide berth.

"What's your problem?" he said. She'd been a colleague of his for almost three years but had never been civil enough to give him anything more than a grunt or a cursory nod whenever he'd greeted her. He didn't know why. Maybe he should.

"Oh, you'll find out," she said cheerily.

Oliver sat down in a leather chair across the desk from his boss. Roger had his head bent down, scribbling something into a file. A strand of the gray comb-over that did little to hide the gaping bald spot on the top of his head sprang loose and dangled near his ear. Without skipping a beat, he tucked it behind his ear, set the pen down, and slowly looked at Oliver.

"Do you know why you're here?" Roger said.

Oliver wracked his brain. In the three years, he'd been with Bell, he'd never been written up for anything. A few of his colleagues had even commented that he was one of the better customer service reps. Customer ratings, surveys, and recordings had certainly indicated that. But since fantasy woman, Selina, had appeared six months ago, and since his maniacal obsession with her had begun two months ago, he knew he'd started to let a few things slide. But what exactly had sparked this?

"Not really," Oliver said.

Roger stared daggers. "Really. Well, you should know."

"I can't read your mind, you know." *Keep the sarcasm down. This is your job you're talking about.*

"I'm not asking you to read my mind." Roger's tone was cold and indifferent. "I plan on telling you what the problem is. I was gonna try and put this politely, but I don't really like your attitude right now, so I'm not gonna sugar-coat it. Basically, the problem is this: you stink."

"I thought I was one of the better customer service reps."

"I'm not talking about your job performance. I'm talking about your personal hygiene. When was the last time you had a shower? And I know in this day and age I'm not supposed to tell people how to wear their hair anymore, but screw it, I will anyway. When was the last time you got a haircut?"

Reflexively, maybe instinctively, Oliver raised his arm and sniffed. A salty, musty odor assaulted his nostrils, one he'd evidently become all too familiar—and comfortable—with. He quickly replayed the weekend over in his mind. After the Saturday night slasher nightmare, he'd stayed up most of the night vicariously enjoying another horror movie marathon and plenty of junk food. He'd slept most of the day on Sunday (a deep Selina-less and slasher-less sleep) and that night pulled another late-night horror movie shift at the TV with a six-pack of Coke, six bags of chips, a half dozen donuts, and four large chocolate bars. He hadn't gotten to bed until 4:30 am and, waking for work two and a half hours later, he simply hadn't the time to shower. He'd barely managed a half-assed shave. He thought he'd pulled up his T-shirt and splashed some water on his pits, but maybe he'd even forgotten to do that. So, it was going on four days since he'd had a shower. *Shit. No, you smell like shit.*

Roger interrupted Oliver's introspection. "Look, you don't have to answer those questions. It's obvious it's been a few days. Your co-workers are starting to notice. And this isn't the first time they've complained to me about it."

Oliver focused on another errant strand of hair that had freed itself from his boss's comb-over. It dangled about three inches below his ear, swinging gently to and fro. Oliver wondered when—it wasn't a question of if—Roger would realign it with the others, futilely trying to hide the lustrous sheen on the top of his head. *Probably after I leave. For sure after you leave.*

Roger pushed himself away from the desk. His captain's chair rolled back and clinked against the large window behind him. "Did I grow horns or something? Why are you staring at me like that? Don't you have anything to say for yourself?"

"I'm sorry, boss. I promise to pay more attention to my personal hygiene from now on."

"I'd certainly appreciate that. Because you're not a bad employee and I'd hate to have to let you go." Roger let the words sink in for a moment before continuing. "You'll have to forgive me for asking this, but is there any history of mental illness in your family? Do you personally have any mental illness in your past?"

Why does he always ask at least two questions at once? "Not that I know of." Oliver's biological parents had both died of tragic illnesses when he was only three years old. He never had any brothers or sisters, at least none he knew about. He'd later been adopted by Mallory, his mother's sister. She'd raised him with a firm hand and a lot of love. Unfortunately, when he was only nineteen, she died of cancer. Since then, Oliver had been on his own. He knew he had other relatives somewhere in England but hadn't bothered to look them up.

"What, you mean your family or yourself?"

"Both," Oliver said, unwilling to elaborate.

"Okay, sorry. I had to ask. We do have psychologists and social workers here. If you have some personal problem that you don't feel I'm qualified to handle, or you don't want to discuss with me, I can always refer you to one of our specialists."

"Thanks, but I'm fine."

"Are you? You don't look fine, Oliver."

For a moment, Oliver didn't know what to say. He couldn't tell Roger about Selina. His boss would think him nuts. But, he had to say something. Or did he? An excuse popped into his mind. "I've just been having trouble sleeping lately. Been thinking I'd like to have a girlfriend but can't seem to meet anyone."

"Well, if you cleaned yourself up a bit that would be a good start."

"Okay, boss. I'll do that. I promise." Oliver was beginning to feel nervous and slightly embarrassed that he had let it come to this. He wanted to get out of that office ASAP. "Can I go back to work now?"

"No."

Oliver froze. A bead of sweat popped on his forehead and he was too catatonic to wipe it away. "What, you mean you're firing me?"

"No. I can't let you return to work in your... in your condition. I'm sending you home now. Come back tomorrow, and please look a little more presentable. I mean a lot more presentable."

Oliver lifted his 240-pound mass from the chair. It creaked. He turned to go.

"Oliver?"

He turned around.

"Are you sure there isn't anything myself or one of our specialists can help you with?"

"I'm... I'm sure."

"Fine... I almost forgot. You know we have a fully equipped exercise gym in the building, don't you?"

"Yeah, I know that."

"I'm just saying. Exercise not only improves your physical well-being, it also improves your mental health."

You saying I'm a nutcase? I think he is. "Thanks, I'll think about it. See you tomorrow, boss. Thanks for not firing me."

"Where are you going?" Frannie asked, giving Oliver a wide berth as he scooped up a brown knapsack that contained his massive lunch. "It's only eleven o'clock."

Oliver bit his tongue to prevent saying something nasty. "I'm going home. See you tomorrow."

Frannie ignored the comment and pressed a flashing button on the phone console in front of her. "Good morning, Bell Canada Customer Service Department. How can I help you today?"

Driving home in his 1993 Toyota Tercel a few minutes later, Oliver's mind clung to the last words Roger had said to him before he'd left the office. *"I'm just saying. Exercise not only improves your physical well-being, it also improves your mental health."*

Improves my mental health? Does he think I've lost my mind? Have I lost my mind? Does he think I'm depressed? Am I depressed? Jesus Christ, I better start figuring some shit out.

Yeah, you better.

Chapter Four

Oliver looked across the dinner table at Carmen Weathersby with mixed emotions. During the pre-dinner conversation, she'd exhibited a vulnerability and sensitivity that he found endearing. He even liked her pleasing plumpness and the cute way she brushed that pesky lock of curly brown hair away from her face before she spoke. Finley had given him a little backstory, except to say she was shy and reserved until she got to know you and had been unsuccessful in relationships. And, while he found her to be reserved initially, he also noticed two glasses of red wine had created a blossoming red rose.

Yet she wasn't Selina and that fact bothered him. Would Selina get jealous of his... infidelity? He didn't know, but he was also reluctant to take any chances. Even though, after Roger's warning at work last week, he'd gone some way to cleaning himself up, even going as far as showering, shaving, and getting a haircut. But his apartment was another story. He felt like one of those hoarders on a reality show who, coddled by a hoarding-specialist psychologist, had only managed to clear one square foot of clutter in a week.

"Where do you live?" Carmen asked, setting her glass of wine on the table. "What's your apartment like?"

Right on cue. It unnerved Oliver. "It's a small apartment just outside the downtown core. Nothing fancy." *Divert. Deflect.* "How about you? Where do you live?"

Ruby, a thin and attractive woman with long sandy-brown hair, rose from the table, scooped up some cutlery and a few plates, and gave her husband Finley a look. Finley took the cue, removed a few items from the table, and followed her into the kitchen.

Oliver got the message. They were leaving the two alone to let them bond. Dealing with the dishes ostensibly, but certainly not dealing with the kids. Oliver knew they were at Ruby's mother's for the weekend, the couple's stand-in babysitter.

"I live with my mom not far from here," Carmen said. "Scarborough. She's ninety-five. Instead of putting her in a nursing home, I decided to look after her in my childhood home. It's a wreck of an old home, but in an excellent location in the downtown core. Just the land is probably worth over a million."

"That's very caring of you."

"I wish it was just that," Carmen said. "But I can't afford an apartment in this city on my salary. Mom charges a pittance in lieu of my nursing duties. How do you afford your home? Finley said you work as a customer service rep for Bell. That can't pay that much."

"I was lucky enough to find government-subsidized housing a long time ago. My rent is based on my income and it's cheap."

"Lucky you," Carmen said, twirling the unruly lock of hair. She admired the renovated dining room of Ruby and Finley's 1900-built inner-city home. It opened up into an expansive living room decorated with contemporary abstract art and cushy tan leather furniture. Warm brown paint swathed both the dining and living rooms. They'd purchased it before the real estate boom in Toronto and Finley had gutted it to the studs and completely remodeled it.

"Such a beautiful house they have," Carmen said. "I mean, this place must be worth at least two million dollars. We'd never be able to own a place like this on our salaries."

"Not anytime soon," Oliver said. He was about to add, "But when your mom passes, you might," but bit his tongue.

"You were gonna say something?" Carmen asked.

She's intuitive. Damn intuitive. "I was just gonna say at least you live in an inner-city character home now and have cheap rent."

"I do," Carmen said. "But it'll never be mine if that's what you're thinking."

"No, I wasn't," Oliver lied.

"I have one brother and one sister and Mom already told me her estate will be split evenly amongst us. Not that I think about that, you know, but Mom wanted us all to know that."

"It might give you a down payment for a nice condo," Oliver said. He tried to keep his mind focused on the conversation at hand but found it wandering to Selina and what she might be doing and thinking. It occurred to him that, although he'd conjured up an image of what Selina might look like—statuesque, beautiful, curvy, soulful eyes, long black hair—he'd never actually seen that form in his dreams. Other than a sleek black, gravity-defying form, his recollection of her was only in his mind's eye. Watching Carmen, he absently drained his half-full glass of wine. Her brown hair precipitously turned black and grew shoulder-length, a beautiful mane. Her eyes darkened and shone and searched his soul. She grinned and licked her sumptuous and full lips and shook her index finger at Oliver.

"You shouldn't be here."

"What?" he said, starting and knocking over his empty wine glass, staring at Carmen in shock. "What did you say?"

"I said would you like a beer?" Ruby's voice. Behind him. "I know you're not much of a wine drinker."

Oliver felt the color drain from his face and his heart skip a beat. He scrubbed his new brush cut with a hand and turned to Ruby. "Ah, I'll have a Coke if you have it."

"I do," Ruby said, then turning to Carmen. "How about you, my dear?"

Oliver noticed the color had also drained from Carmen's cheeks but was relieved to see she no longer resembled Selina. But the red rose was wilting. *She must've read my shock, read my fear. Shit. Oh yes. She did. You're fucked now.*

"Just a glass of water," Carmen said.

Ruby scooped up a few more dishes and disappeared into the kitchen, leaving the two to deal with the uncomfortable silence that had abruptly blanketed the room.

Oliver squirmed in his chair. "I'm sorry."

"For what?"

"I... I think you know."

"What... what do I know?"

"What did you see in me... to suddenly turn so white?"

"I don't know... some dark presence. Some fear, mixed with an attraction, mixed with shock, mixed with some strange longing. I think the better question is what did you see in me that triggered what I saw in you?"

Oliver knew it was not the time or place to bring up Selina. Hell, the woman of his dreams, in his dreams, had already shown up uninvited. In spite of his reservations, he'd decided he liked Carmen. The last thing he wanted to do was convince her that he was batshit crazy, even though he probably was.

Make up something and make it quick. "When you mentioned your mom, I just started thinking about my own parents and it made me sad. They died of terrible illnesses when I was only three. I was an only child raised by Mallory, my mom's sister."

"I'm sorry," Carmen said, although Oliver could tell she didn't look convinced.

"It was a long time ago," Oliver said. "But thanks."

Another long and uncomfortable silence followed, finally broken by the appearance of Ruby and Finley, chatting amicably while they served chocolate cake for dessert. Before they'd entered, Oliver had decided to leave before Selina reappeared again, but the chocolate cake, resurrecting his junk-food-junkie demons, convinced him otherwise. He gobbled up three large servings before thanking his friends for dinner, telling Carmen what a pleasure it'd been to meet her, and bidding everyone farewell.

He watched her watch him leave, both white-faced.

Driving home, his hands started shaking uncontrollably at the wheel and he pulled over to calm his nerves. *Damn. I really need to get a grip.* Taking deep breaths, he sat on his hands to try and still the jittering while he reflected on the dinner. Everything had been going well until Selina had forced her presence upon him. Selina inside of Carmen. What did it mean? Was Carmen really Selina? Or was Selina possessing Carmen to reach him? To discourage him from pursuing Carmen. That was the more likely scenario, Oliver decided, especially when considered in the context of her warning: *"You shouldn't be here."*

He ran several scenarios through his mind, grappling with how to handle the aftermath of these strange and mysterious events. *Should I call Carmen and tell her the truth? No, out of the question. Should I call her and apologize for my sudden mood change? You don't even have her number. But, I can get it. Finley will give it to me. Maybe not. Maybe not without Carmen's permission.* Then the answer did come to him. And it was so simple he was stunned he didn't see it earlier. He didn't even know if Carmen liked him. Maybe she was just being polite and civil. He could call Finley tomorrow and find out if any future contact with her was even possible. But, he still had to deal with the Selina issue. He removed his hands from underneath his legs and studied them. They were steady and unwavering. He grinned nervously and decided he knew just how to do that.

He turned the key in the ignition. *Click.*

There was a rap on the window.

Oliver jerked, craning his neck swiftly to get a look at his attacker before it was too late.

"No, no, Selina, I'm sorry."

The man backed away and reached for his gun. Then in a split-second, he removed his hand from the holster and twirled his finger, motioning for Oliver to roll the window down. Seeing the flashing red lights in his rear-view mirror, Oliver realized it was a cop. He rolled his window down.

The flashlight-carrying cop, silhouetted by blackness, features barely discernable, spoke: "You okay, mister?"

"Yeah."

"What the hell were you saying, anyway? I'm not Selina. You break up with your girlfriend or something?"

Oliver had the excuse he wanted. "We, uh, had a fight. I just pulled over to calm my nerves."

"Well, you can't park here. It's too dangerous. And it's illegal. Get a move on."

"I... I was just leaving, officer. Sorry. Thanks."

Oliver was relieved the cop hadn't decided to put him through the third degree—driver's license, run the tags, an interrogation, maybe a ticket—so he quickly started the car, signaled and shoulder-checked, and pulled away.

"You go straight home now," the cop said as Oliver cautiously merged into evening traffic.

Chapter Five

Carmen watched Sarah, her mother, lying in bed, a mere shadow of her former self. Ninety-five pounds. Ninety-five years old. Frail and weak. A deteriorating memory. Repeating the same stories over and over and over again. Forgetting when had taken the painkillers Carmen gave her every four hours for arthritic knees. Forgetting what day it was, what time it was, what she had done yesterday, and what she had done today. *How cruel life can be; slowly stripping us of all awareness of who we once were. Sitting on death's doorstep, on the edge of terror and horror, realizing every breath we take might be our last.*

Carmen shook two pills from a Tylenol bottle, put one in a spoon, and put the spoon to her mother's wrinkled lips. "Here you go, Mom."

Sarah eyed Carmen soulfully with an expression that almost begged for it to be over and managed a weak smile. She opened her mouth and, using the spoon, Carmen placed a pill on her mother's tongue and handed her a glass of water.

Sarah drank and swallowed and Carmen repeated the procedure with the other pill.

Sarah cleared her throat and pulled the blanket up over her shoulders, her long gray hair falling over her sunken face. "It's cold in here. Can you turn the heat up?"

"Mom, the heat is at eighty."

"Is it?"

"Yeah."

"Just a little. Please."

"Okay, Mom."

"You forgot, you know?"

"Forgot? Forgot what?"

"The painkillers. I haven't had any all day. My knees hurt."

With a sigh, Carmen sat down on the chair beside the bed. "Mom, I gave you two before I left for dinner four hours ago. And two just now."

"You what?"

Carmen raised her voice. "Mom, I gave you two before I left for dinner. Four hours ago. And two more just now."

"You did?"

"Yes."

"Okay, my memory is getting bad."

"It's okay."

"How was your date?" Sarah asked.

Carmen moved the chair closer to her mother and leaned forward. Although her hearing was getting worse, Sarah had stubbornly refused to wear a hearing aid.

"It wasn't really a date, Mom. It was dinner with some friends."

"I thought you said you were meeting a new boy."

"I did. He was there."

"Well, at least in my generation, that's called a date."

"Okay."

"Well, don't keep me in suspense. How was it? How is this new guy?"

Carmen knew she had to sugar-coat it a little, if not a lot. In the beginning, she had thought Oliver was a weirdo. But as the evening progressed, she'd started to warm to him. His honesty. His vulnerability, even his fragile confidence. Such a wounded soul, much like herself. But, after Ruby and Finley had left them to their own devices, things had taken a turn for the worse. When he'd looked at her like she was a she-devil, she'd felt it too. A dark and pervasive presence had swept over her, terrifying in its forcefulness. And that had changed her mind. Driving home, she'd decided she wanted nothing to do with him. And if he asked for her number through Finley and Ruby, she'd politely decline with a simple explanation, *"Nice guy, but not my type."*

"I don't know."

"What do you mean you don't know? Is that all there is? Is he at least good looking?"

"I don't find him ugly. He's a big man with a baby face."

"But not your type?"

Should I tell her? She's at the end of her road. Why not? Sarah possessed the innate intuitiveness of the supernatural that none of Carmen's siblings possessed. As a child, Carmen remembered the phone ringing on several occasions and her mother knew who it was before she'd even answered. She did not have a call display.

And she had a sixth sense when it came to supernatural events. She'd often claimed she could feel the presence of a spectral entity in the house, but her sense was that Melvin the ghost was a kind and gentle soul who, after passing away, simply wanted to remain in his childhood home. At times, Carmen also sensed Melvin's presence but it wasn't strong enough to evoke emotions one way or the other. She did detect, however, that her mother's knowledge of the supernatural was far greater than she let on. Maybe she wanted to shield her children from the dangers and fear that might be associated with knowing too much.

So surely there was no harm in some motherly advice. Her mother had never steered her wrong in the past. Quite the contrary. Her intuitions concerning her other boyfriends had always hit the nail on the head with a brutally accurate clarity of vision.

"I don't think so, Mom. What do you think?"

"About what?"

"About Oliver?"

"I haven't even met him."

"But you usually know."

After a short silence, Sarah said, "First tell me your impression."

"At first I thought he was a weirdo. Then I warmed to him a bit. But during dinner, he looked at me like he'd seen a ghost, like I was the ghost, and it scared the crap out of me."

Sarah scratched her chin. Her eyes rolled around the dimly lit room, stopped at the blind-covered window for a moment, and then continued their journey to Carmen, stopping at her eyes. Her mother let out a deep sigh, crinkled her brow, and closed her eyes.

"What, Mom? Don't keep me in suspense. What do you think of him?"

Sarah opened her eyes and locked them onto her daughter. "I think he's a lost soul who needs serious help."

"What about the dark presence? Do you feel anything?"

"I thought I did, but it's gone, whatever it was."

"Am I the one to help him? Should I help him?"

"I don't know right now. I'm tired. Maybe I'll know something by tomorrow."

"Okay." Carmen leaned over, kissed her mother on the cheek, and stood up.

Sarah pulled the blankets halfway up her face. "Don't forget to turn the heat up."

Carmen sighed deeply. "Okay. Do you want the light out, Mom?"

"Please. The little nightlight will do."

Carmen turned the bedside lamp off and left the room, closing the door gently behind her. In the hallway, she turned the thermostat up a few degrees, even though it was the middle of summer.

Sitting on the couch in the living room drinking an iced tea a few minutes later, she absently channel-surfed, seeing but not seeing the colorful images flashing before her. What her mother had said had troubled her and she needed time to think about it. Sarah had felt something. Carmen had felt something. Surely this must be a sign to give Oliver a wide berth. Whatever had attached itself to him must be a mysterious and malevolent force. Something to be feared. Something to be respected. And something to stay the hell away from. After a few more minutes of contemplation, she finished her iced tea and made her way upstairs to bed. In the bedroom and in front of a full-length wall-mounted mirror, she stripped down to her bra and panties and took a few moments to admire her oversized, voluptuous body. It had never bothered her in the past that her body didn't resemble that of an anorexic supermodel. She was big-boned and had some meat on her bones. Some men, at least the ones she was interested in, liked her just the way she was. Her mind drifted back to Oliver and she remembered the way he'd undressed her with his eyes when they'd first met. Sure, he'd tried to do it discreetly, but his examination was certainly not missed on Carmen. And she knew one thing for sure, he'd liked what he saw.

She brought her hands to her large breasts and cupped them, pushing them upward and trying to decide if a push-up bra might make her more desirous to men. But, after moving closer to the mirror and studying her breasts from different angles, she decided they were fine just the way they were. After all, she was a size 40DD. It's not like men would miss them.

She bent down to turn off the bedside lamp and caught her reflection in the mirror, backdropped by a black shadow, something she hadn't noticed earlier. The shadow enveloped her reflection and, just for s second, she saw her naked body much differently than it really was. She was tall and curvy and a lot less plump. Her breasts were large and firm, gravity-defying, and her derriere was curvaceous but tight, half the size of her real one. Her once short, curly hair had transformed to long and black. Her mouth dropped open and, horrified, she quickly switched off the light and jumped into bed, pulling the covers up all the way over her face. Taking quick breaths, she tried to calm herself, saying over and over, "It's your mind playing tricks on you. Open your eyes and everything will be gone."

And sure enough, after five minutes of convincing herself nothing had happened, she opened her eyes and surveyed the room. The same flowery wallpaper dimly illuminated by the moonlight seeping in from the sheer blinds. The same nightlight glowing dully from an outlet beside an antique oak dresser. The wall-mounted mirror reflected a sliver of moonlight, tinted yellow from the nightlight. Her hands roamed her body. Good. Bra and panties still in place and her butt and breasts the same size that God had gifted her with.

She sighed. "Go away, dark spirit, go away, forever."

And, as an extra layer of protection, she closed her eyes and prayed silently, a devout Christian that she was. "Please, God, if any evil spirit has invaded my body, or invaded the body of Oliver, banish it forever. Thank you, Lord. Amen."

Opening her eyes, she felt better. God would protect her from evil. He always had before. As fatigue gave way to a relaxed slumber and consciousness ebbed away, her last thoughts wandered back to Oliver. In some ways, she thought the whole set-up was silly and cliché, maybe even a romance novel trope. Two heartbroken souls, both psychologically scarred from previous relationships, meet, confront their demons, fall in love, and live happily ever after.

She guessed that Finley and Ruby would've provided Oliver with some of her backstory, at least regarding what they thought they knew. What they didn't know was it wasn't entirely true. People made assumptions based on your relationship history. They assumed you were heartbroken, tainted, and messed up. Actually, Carmen was happy to be rid of the previous assholes in her life. And she was convinced her therapist had exorcised her demons, making her ready, willing, and quite emotionally able for another relationship.

As she drifted off into the black void of unconsciousness, the last thought crossed her mind: *But not with him. No, not with him.*

Chapter Six

I want to be with him. Yes, him. He's the one. Arms wrapped tightly around her legs, Stella sat in the black void of nothingness and prayed and hoped for the apparition to return. When she'd heard its voice for the first time, her apathy and anger had once again returned to hope and longing. *It spoke. He spoke. "I can only help you if you help yourself."*

But how? How do I help myself? The more she ruminated about it, the more she understood that something wasn't quite the same, wasn't quite right. Lately, she'd begun to sense another being in the void, another woman. She'd even tried speaking to her a few times but had been met with silence. How she knew it was another woman, she didn't know. But, she knew. And she also knew the woman wasn't a permanent resident here. Stella had sensed her presence, and she'd also detected when the woman wasn't here. She'd leave for periods of time and then return to a spot somewhere in the distance, just out of physical reach, but certainly within sensory perception. And there was something else Stella detected about the woman. Something dark. She had a malicious agenda. She couldn't put a finger on exactly what that agenda was, but she knew it wasn't good. Then another thought occurred to her. Was this woman getting in the way of her happiness? Was she interfering with him? She better not be.

The black void abruptly became cold and Stella felt the dark presence seeping into it. A cold chill brushed the nape of her neck and she shuddered. She opened her eyes but could only see blackness.

"You stepping on my territory?" Stella said, standing up, and surprised that she could. It was usually a sinkhole.

Instead of a voice, she heard a low hissing sound, straight ahead, maybe fifty feet.

"Speak to me," she said, stepping forward on protesting joints. "You messing with what's not rightfully yours?"

"It's not yours," a voice said. "It's mine."

Stella's blood boiled. She clenched her fists.

Out of the blackness, a long-haired statuesque woman in a black bodysuit appeared, backlit by a soft, yellow glow. She was holding something. A whip, maybe?

Stella gritted her teeth and charged, shocked by the speed and agility with which she was thrust forward, advancing on long-dormant bones and muscles.

She hit the woman hard in the mid-section, putting her entire shoulder into the body blow. She heard the hissing sound of air escaping as the woman fell back, winded, the two of them rolling on a spongy black surface. Stella landed on top of the woman, tore the whip out of her hands, and flung it aside. She then brought both hands down and began strangling the woman with such unbridled rage that the woman's head jerked up and down.

"You die," Stella said, mystified that she could not yet see any facial features on the woman. Her face was a mask of blackness.

The woman brought a hand up and placed it squarely over Stella's face.

"No, no," Stella shouted as the hand closed around her face, blocking her vision.

In a swift motion, the woman squeezed hard and, headfirst, flung Stella off her. Panting for breath but yet evidently energized by the sudden attack, she sprang to her feet and moved purposefully toward Stella.

Stella wiped what she believed was blood from her nose and tried to scramble to her feet. One foot sank in the ooze. She tried the other foot with the same result.

The woman bent down, retrieved her whip, and continued forward. "You're not going anywhere. You're stuck in a quagmire of your own making."

"What... what do you mean, my making? You're... you're the evil one."

But the first crack of the whip across the face silenced Stella. She was now up to her knees in shit, still sinking, and grappling for some kind of a hand-hold. And as the dark woman stepped in closer and raised the whip for another strike, Stella found it. With both hands, she reached out and grabbed the woman's ankle, yanking on it with all her strength. The woman tripped and fell, coming down hard. Stella crawled up the ankle, noticing as she did the ground beneath her hardening. Using the woman's leg as a life-saving rope, she crawled out of the sinkhole.

Stella scrambled to her feet, raised her heel high in the air, and lowered it forcefully, aiming for the head. But, just before her foot made contact with the woman's face, she started sinking into the black abyss.

Using her forward momentum, Stella dove forward as the woman now reached for her ankle. For a horrifying split-second, she felt cold tendrils wrap around her ankle, but then her forward thrusting motion shook the hand free and the woman plummeted down the hole.

Stella fell forward, bringing both hands up quickly to cushion her fall. She hit the ground, rolled over on her side, got up on all fours, and crawled over to the hole. Peering down, she saw the woman's twisting, turning, body in free-fall as it dropped into a fiery abyss.

Only when the body disappeared and the woman's screams faded to nothing did Stella exhale deeply and begin to realize just how close she'd come to dying.

She sat back and watched the hole slowly close. When it did, she crawled back on all fours to the familiar discomfort of her corner, the cornerstone of her existence, in the corner of nowhere. However, she was thankful to be alive.

But am I alive? Have I ever been alive?

She curled up into a fetal position, closed her eyes, and waited for her heartbeat to return to normal. As her breathing settled, she decided that tomorrow was another day. And tomorrow she would dedicate herself to the task of discovering who she really was, or who she really had been.

Chapter Seven

Waking up Sunday morning, Oliver was disappointed that he hadn't dreamt about Selina. Even though last night his experience with her, or Carmen turning into her, had been anything but positive. He still hoped to find her in his fantasyland and explain to her that Carmen meant nothing to him. Wait a second. It was only last night when he'd pulled over on the shoulder of the road trembling with fear that he'd formulated a course of action: talk to Finley and Ruby about whether or not Carmen even had an inkling of interest in him.

Returning to his old habits, he'd frittered away most of the day binge-watching horror shows and munching on junk food. Again, he hadn't even bothered to shower, but at the very least he'd made a mental note to himself to rise an hour earlier tomorrow morning and properly clean himself up for work. He didn't want to face the alternative—Fired—and out looking for work with little in the way of marketable skills.

He wolfed down the remainder of his Puritan canned beef stew—he'd never been much of a cook—and reached for his phone. It was coming up five in the afternoon. Surely Finley would know something by now.

Finley answered on the third ring. "What's up, bro?"

Oliver came straight to the point. "What... what did Carmen think of me?"

After an uncomfortable silence, Finley said, "I don't know what happened. I mean, you seemed to be doing fine up until the time Ruby and I left the room. We returned to a cold room, the tension so thick you could slice it with a knife."

Carmen. Selina. Carmen. Selina. Carmen. "Did she say anything to you?"

"Not to me. To Ruby."

"What did she say?"

"She called earlier today to thank us for dinner. Ruby asked her what she thought of you. It's not that bad, really, and I wouldn't necessarily lose hope."

"Come on, already. Spit it out."

"She said you're a nice guy, but not her type."

"Well, she's not my type either."

Now it was Finley's turn. "Come on, already. If you weren't interested in her you wouldn't have asked right off the hop what she thought of you."

Oliver had to admit, his friend had him there. Never mind. It wouldn't go over well with Selina anyway. "I was just curious, that's all."

"Yeah, right. You like her. Admit it."

"It's too early to tell on a first date, but yeah, I did find her attractive."

"What happened anyway, when we left the room?"

Oliver realized Finley didn't much like conversations about Selina. But why lie? His friend probably already considered him a loser and sometimes Oliver wondered what redeeming qualities Finley even saw in him. "I don't know, I guess I need to get out more. For a second, she started to resemble the woman of my dreams."

"You mean the woman in your dreams."

"Right."

"You kidding me?" Finley said. "What, she suddenly transformed into the woman in your dreams?"

"That's about right."

"Holy shit. You're not still dreaming about her, are you?"

"Not lately."

"Have you thought about seeing someone?"

"I thought that's what you were helping me with."

"Uh... that's not what I meant."

"What, you mean like a shrink?"

"Psychiatrist, psychologist, group therapy—whatever you think you need."

"It's you who think I need."

"Well, I tried to set you up with someone I believed you'd have a lot in common with and it turns out she morphs into one of your fantasy women."

"Not one. The one."

"That's exactly what I mean. It sounds like you're obsessed with the woman in your dreams."

Oliver started to realize that Finley might be on to something. But his obsession had gone on far too long for him to abandon it over one suggestion. It would be like trying to convince an alcoholic to quit drinking cold turkey by simply telling him once that he was an alcoholic. Possible, but not very likely. And besides, Oliver still hoped on some level he would consummate his relationship with Selina. He wasn't about to delete the faint hope clause from his contract with craziness. Not yet, anyway, not until he found out where it was gonna go. *Straight to the white padded room with a straitjacket.*

"I'll think about it," Oliver said, hoping to move on to a lighter topic. "What're you up to today?"

"Ruby and I were doing some gardening earlier. I gotta leave to pick up the kids in about ten minutes. How about you?"

"Fuck all. Watching movies and munching."

"Again? Why don't you get outside? It's a beautiful day. Get some fresh air."

"Okay, hey, thanks again for trying to set me up with Selina... err, Carmen. And thanks for dinner."

"Don't mention it. Get some fresh air. Clear your head. And, besides, it's not over until the fat lady sings. Maybe Carmen will have a change of heart."

"I hope so."

"I gotta go."

Oliver put his phone down on the kitchen table—he wouldn't have to worry about missing a call from Carmen—and went into the living room. The TV was still turned on and piercing screams punctuated his entrance as a slasher sliced his way through his latest female victim. Uninterested, Oliver clicked the TV off, grabbed a light jacket, and went outside. After five minutes of walking, he picked a quiet residential street and turned down it. He remembered it led to a small park, an open green space that would give him a chance to figure out his next moves. It was beginning to dawn on him that if he were to have any chance of breaking his vicious cycle—Selina, horror movies, junk food addiction—he would have to stop being in denial about it and at some point confront his demons. Five more minutes of walking and he arrived at the park. As if to remind him of his problems, a couple sat on a blanket at the edge of the park, a cooler in front of them. Oblivious to the law, they sipped beers. In between sips, they exchanged kisses, some of them getting downright passionate.

Oliver did his best to avoid staring at them. He moved as far away from them as possible, clear to the other end of the park, where he found a vacant picnic table. He sat down, noticing right away the nearest person to him was a man sitting on another picnic table about forty feet away, talking to a paper-wrapped bottle and occasionally swilling from it. The disheveled, trenchcoat-wearing man acknowledged Oliver with a nod and a grunt and then returned to his bottle as Oliver sat down and made a point to look the other way.

The bright setting sun, the birds chirping, the magnificent oak trees dotting the park, the green, well-manicured lawn did manage to whisk him away from his problems for a few minutes. He soaked up the sun's warmth and watched the birds flying to and fro. He saw a large black squirrel watching him curiously from a tree as if deciding whether he was friend or foe. The squirrel darted down the tree, raced across the lawn, and stopped about four feet in front of Oliver, chattering loudly.

"What do you want, little guy? I don't have any peanuts. Sorry."

The squirrel watched him for another second, turned, and darted away, making his way up another tree in record time.

Oliver closed his eyes and laid down on top of the picnic table. *What to do? What to do? Should I give up on Selina? I don't know. I don't know if I can.* After thinking about it for about ten minutes, he decided on a compromise. If he didn't see Selina in his dreams for the next seven days—by next Sunday—he would abandon her. He tried to stop his thoughts there, not wanting to entertain the alternative. But questions did surface. What if he did see her in that period? How would he contact her? How would he bring her to life?

A gruff male voice interrupted his contemplation. "Don't give up on her. She's real."

Startled, he opened his eyes, sat up, and saw the bottle-wielding drunk standing in front of him, staring at him curiously.

"What did you say?"

"She's real. Don't give up on her."

"Who's real?"

"And her name's not Selina. It's Stella."

Oliver's jaw dropped. What the fuck? "Selina... I mean, Stella's real?"

"Fucking aye, she is." With that, the man spun around, wobbled on shaky legs for a moment, then found his footing and marched purposefully away.

"Wait," Oliver said. "Come back."

Chapter Eight

Although Sunday evening had been uneventful, Oliver had gone through most of Monday in a daze. He'd barely noticed his colleagues ogling him with more curiosity and intrigue than in the past, perhaps because they now understood he did have the capacity for change. Facing a do-or-die situation, he had started taking an interest in his personal hygiene, at least to the point where he could get through the day without being fired or ratted out by one of his co-workers. He finished his last customer service call and glanced at the clock. Five to five. The day had flown by, as time tends to do when one is preoccupied. He arranged some files on his desk, put a few items in a drawer, and stood, stretching and yawning at the same time. He then reached for his summer jacket.

Others were already filing out of the office, seemingly unconcerned about their early departure. A young freckle-faced woman approached Oliver.

"You done for the day?" She pointed at Oliver's desk, which he knew would be her desk in his absence.

"Go ahead," he said, turning toward the door.

"Don't do it," she said. "Don't contact her."

Oliver was surprised. *Not another one.* "Contact who? What're you talking about?"

Out in the brightly sunlit street, he wiped his tired eyes. He'd decided to leave his vehicle at home today and experience public transit for a rare change. It would give him a chance to mingle with humanity instead of his junk food and TV. He started walking toward the bus stop, weaving absently in and out of pedestrians on the crowded streets.

Beep...beep... beep.

"Hey, Oliver."

He spun around, startled. A black newer model Hyundai Accent pulled curbside and the passenger door flipped open. Carmen motioned to him from the driver seat. "Need a ride?"

"I dunno."

"Well, make up your mind. I'll have cars honking at me in no time."

Oliver climbed in and closed the door. Carmen checked her mirror and merged into busy Toronto traffic, ignoring the blasting of two car horns from angry motorists behind her.

"See," she said. "These impatient bastards won't let you stop for two seconds. Good thing you got in now before one of those wankers pulled a baseball bat out, worse still a fucking gun or something like that."

Oliver was speechless. After everything he'd heard, what the hell was Carmen doing picking him up from work?

But Carmen didn't give him a lot of time for introspection. "We need to talk. I know what you saw that night at Ruby and Finley's. I know what you saw in me. I saw it too and I wanna know what the hell's going on."

"But... but..."

"Oh, no. No buts. We're going for coffee and we're gonna hash this out. My mother warned me this morning before I left for work. She thinks someone is possessing you and by default also trying to possess me."

"Wh... what did you see?"

"Wait until we get where we're going. Where do you wanna have coffee?"

Oliver named a Tim Horton's coffee and donut shop that was a few blocks from where he lived. He gave Carmen some quick directions and watched her silently as she weaved her way through traffic for about ten minutes and finally pulled into the parking lot.

"This is it, right?"

"Yeah."

Standing in the lineup inside the Tim Horton's, Oliver said, "Why don't you find us a seat and I'll buy."

"Okay."

"What do you want?"

"Large coffee. One cream, one sugar."

He watched Carmen walk away, turn down a crowded booth-filled aisle and stop in front of a young couple who were clearing their table and preparing to leave. Carmen waited patiently for them to get up before sliding into an empty, cushioned bench seat.

Oliver felt a nudge on his shoulder and turned around.

"You're next, buddy," a man said. "Over there."

"Sorry."

The man ignored him and Oliver spotted the empty cashier and approached as the woman rolled her eyes. Ever since Carmen had picked him up, the confusion he'd felt during work that day had only intensified. His mind was racing a million miles an hour, trying to figure out if Carmen would again morph into, *that's right, Stella,* even before he managed to return with their order.

He paid for the order, unable to resist a box of twenty mini donut balls, found the booth where Carmen sat, and plunked himself down across from her.

"Want a Timbit?" he said, opening the box and popping a chocolate ball into his mouth.

"Not right now," she said. "Thanks for the coffee." She peeled the lid off and took a sip. "You want to know what I saw?"

She isn't wasting time on small talk, Oliver thought, popping another donut in his mouth and washing it down with a sip of coffee.

"Yeah."

"It happened the night of the dinner party after I got home. I was getting ready for bed and I glanced at my reflection. Only it wasn't my reflection. It was a different body style. Tall and shapely, but not fat like me. And long black hair, not short and curly like mine."

"My God," Oliver said before even realizing the words had escaped his lips. He'd planned on bluffing his way through this, but the terrified look on Carmen's face told him in no uncertain terms to level with her.

"Is that what you saw?" Carmen said. "At the dinner party? In me?"

"Well, you weren't nude or anything but your hair and face had definitely changed like you said. It rattled me."

"I knew something rattled you. Who is this woman to you?"

"I'm not sure, but I think she's a woman in my dreams. A fantasy woman who always feels so real."

"Maybe she *is* real," Carmen said. "What does she want with me?"

"I don't know."

"Have you seen her lately?"

That one caught Oliver off guard. "Yeah, in you."

"I meant in your dreams. Before that."

"I don't think I've seen her in my dreams for like a week." He considered mentioning the other woman who'd recently appeared in his dreams: the bikini-bottomed, big breasted blonde armed with a blood-soaked butcher knife, who'd recently attacked him. But, he changed his mind, hoping the two weren't related. Besides, Carmen looked scared enough as it was without injecting more fear inside her. And her question had been very specific. About Selina. No, Stella.

"Have you noticed anything weird happening lately?"

Oliver gobbled another donut. Carmen also reached for one and took a small bite out of it.

"What do you mean?" Oliver said, knowing damn well what she meant.

The drunk in the park. *"Don't give up on her. She's real."*

The woman at work. *"Don't do it. Don't contact her."*

"I mean, people saying weird things, referencing this woman?" Carmen asked.

Oliver relayed the comments from the woman at work and the drunk in the park. He decided there was no point holding out. Stella, evidently her real name, was supposed to be the woman of his dreams, but she was rapidly transforming into a living nightmare.

"He said her name's Stella, if that helps," Oliver added. "The drunk, I mean."

Carmen rolled her eyes deep into the back of her head as if searching internally for some recognition of the name. "Stella. Hmm. That doesn't ring any bells right now."

"Have you heard any strange comments about Stella?" Oliver said. "What did your mother say exactly?"

Carmen set part of her donut on a napkin and took a sip of coffee. "As I said in the car, my mom said she thinks you're being possessed, and by extension so am I. She was the one who told me this morning that by saving you I could save myself. She thinks you, well, wittingly or unwittingly, brought this evil into my life. Other than her comments, I haven't heard anything from anyone else."

"This is all so weird," Oliver said.

"I know," Carmen agreed. "I wish I'd never met you."

Oliver frowned, a grim understanding beginning to settle over him that he was the source, at least the conduit, for evil. "I'd never do anything to harm you. I... I didn't bring this into your life wittingly. I want you to know that." And he blurted it out without thinking. "And Finley already told me I'm not your type, so my interest in you isn't romantic."

"I don't know what you mean by that. What is your interest in me?"

Oliver held both hands up, open-palmed. "Hey, you were the one who picked me up after work."

"Listen, what my mother told me scared me. I don't want you to think for a second I have any romantic interest in you. I'll be honest, my motives are selfish ones. Self-preservationist ones. It's true what Finley said. When I met you at their place I thought in the beginning you were a nice guy, albeit a little weird. Who knows, maybe I did warm to you a little, but you're still not my type. Then that shit happened with... Stella... and after that, I swore to have nothing to do with you."

Oliver reached for another donut. But he withdrew his hand, suddenly losing his appetite. He picked up his coffee and took a sip. "What I was trying to say, and I guess I put my foot in my mouth, is if you think you're in trouble and you need my help I'll do whatever I can to help you. That's my only interest. *Our* self-preservation."

"I wouldn't come to you for help if I didn't believe our fates are inextricably linked," Carmen said.

Carmen's confrontational tone and statements were starting to raise the hairs on Oliver's back. "You don't know that for sure. I mean that our fates are inextricably linked."

"Oh, yes, I do. My mom has never been wrong with her predictions before. She knows a lot about the supernatural."

"Oh yeah, like what?"

Carmen gave Oliver a long look which clearly said don't push your luck with me. "When I was a kid, my mom used to know who was calling before she answered the phone. This was before the days of call display. Or, if they did have it then, we didn't have it. And, she senses things—like extrasensory perception."

"What, like she can tell if a ghost is in the room?"

"Exactly. Do you believe in ghosts?"

"I don't know. Do you?"

"Yeah," Carmen said. "And evil spirits. Anyway, she senses this Melvin ghost whenever he makes his presence felt. I've felt him too. But not as strong as Mom. She knows he means us no harm, so we're content to let him stay in what my mom calls his family home."

"If she senses things maybe she can help us," Oliver said.

"She does and she has already," Carmen said. "I mean she warned me about you and told me how to save myself."

"By saving me?"

"Right."

"And how does she propose to do that?"

Carmen scratched her chin. "I don't know. It was too early in the morning when I spoke to her and I had to get ready for work. The only thing I remembered her saying was I gotta save you to save myself. I thought, well to do that, I definitely have to hook up… I mean see you again."

"But you don't really know how to save me?"

Carmen's brow crinkled. "No, I don't. I was thinking that might be tonight's conversation."

"Why don't I meet her?" Oliver said. "If she has such strong extra sensory perceptions, then maybe by meeting me she'll be able to tell us how to expel this so-called evil."

"You don't think it's evil?"

Now it was Oliver's turn to furrow his brow. "I don't know what it is, Carmen. I'm confused. But, as I said, if you need my help, you've got it."

After a long pause, Carmen said, "Maybe you're right. Why don't you meet my mom tonight? I mean, seriously, I don't think this is something that we can delay."

In spite of the hot, muggy weather, a grizzled, bottle-wielding man entered the coffee shop and marched resolutely toward the booth they occupied.

The booze smell hit Carmen and Oliver before he did.

The man stopped in front of the table and held the bottle high in the air.

Carmen and Oliver cringed. Oliver brought an arm over the table, shielding Carmen's face as she shrank into the corner of the booth.

"Don't delay," the man said. "Contact Stella now. Your lives depend on it."

Before they could speak, he spun around and quickly exited the coffee shop, patron eyes following him.

An annoyed-looking supervisor approached Carmen and Oliver's booth. "Sorry about that," he said. "He's a pain in the ass and I hate when he harasses customers."

"It's okay," Carmen said.

The manager fashioned a plastic smile and returned to his managerial duties.

"That's him," Oliver said, his hands beginning to shake.

"Who?" Carmen asked.

"The drunk in the park."

***

Driving to her house a few minutes later, Carmen glanced at Oliver and said, "Do you like me?"

"Why do you care?" Oliver said. "You don't like me."

"You wouldn't understand these things," she said. "It's a woman's prerogative to want to know."

"Yeah," Oliver said, figuring he had nothing to lose. "I *do* like you."

Carmen smiled, a shock of pink coloring her plump cheeks. "Good. And I didn't say I didn't like you. Just not in that way... you know what I mean."

Oliver nodded. "Do you think I like you in that way?"

"Do you?"

May as well ride the wave, Oliver thought, knowing it was gonna come crashing ashore any second now. "Yeah, I think I do."

But instead of crashing, the wave swelled. "Good."

***

Inside the dimly lit house, Oliver approached Sarah's bedroom with some trepidation. "Are you sure this is okay? I mean, does she even know?"

Carmen took his hand. Her skin was soft and warm to the touch and Oliver liked it.

"She will know soon," Carmen assured him. "Come on. You have any better ideas?"

"Not really," Oliver admitted.

Carmen turned the doorknob and the door creaked open. Dusk was already settling over the city and Sarah's ashen face was barely lit by a few spears of light poking through gaps in the thick red blinds.

Carmen released Oliver's hand and approached the bed. Oliver followed, jumpy.

Sarah's eyes were closed and her shallow chest heaved with labored breaths. She opened her eyes and stared directly at Oliver. "You've come?"

"Yes," Oliver said. "I'm Oliver."

"I... I know," Sarah croaked. "What're you doing to my daughter?"

"Nothing, at least not intentionally. Your daughter thought it would help if I met you. That you could help us."

Carmen stepped forward, leaned down, and put a comforting hand on her mother's shoulder. "Mom, you said I need to save Oliver to save myself. How do I do that? How do we do that?"

Sarah cleared her throat as if to speak, but then slowly closed her eyes. They watched her silently for a few moments until she slowly opened her eyes.

"I feel something," Sarah said. "I feel something strange."

"What is it, Mom? Is it good or bad?"

"Both good and bad," Sarah said. "An evil entity and a good entity is fighting for control of one body. You must contact the good entity to help you expel the evil entity once and for all. If you can do this, you'll save yourselves. If you can't... we're all doomed."

Sarah said it with such conviction and finality that Oliver clasped both of his hands together to prevent them from shaking. *Not again.*

Carmen turned to him. "What're you doing? Praying?"

"No. Trying to stop my hands from shaking."

"Enough," Sarah said with authority and strength that belied her years. "Time is of the essence. There is a key in a jewelry box over here in my bedside drawer. The key opens a steel box in the attic. Inside it, you'll find a doll-shaped talisman. You'll also find an instruction book. Use them to contact the spirit world. Do it. Do it now!"

Oliver watched as what little color Sarah had in her shrunken face drained away. She closed her eyes and in no time began a slow and heavy breathing.

Carmen bent down again and kissed her mother on the forehead. Turning to Oliver, she said, "Come on. It's okay. She's sleeping."

Up on the second floor, Carmen went into a spare bedroom and reappeared in the upper hallway with a chair. She placed it underneath a small attic hatch and gestured to Oliver with a hand. "In this case, shouldn't it be gentlemen before ladies?"

He nodded and climbed up on the chair while Carmen circled behind it, placing one hand on the chair and one hand on Oliver's leg.

"I think I'm okay," Oliver said, beginning to slide the hatch away.

She released his leg and put two hands on the chair.

As he removed the hatch, a plume of dust flew out, powdering them and causing them to cough.

When they'd stopped coughing, Oliver said, "Here," handing the small wooden attic hatch door to Carmen. She took it and leaned it against the wall.

"Can you see anything?" she said.

"No. You got a flashlight?"

She went into the same small bedroom and reappeared a few seconds later with a flashlight. She turned it on and handed it to Oliver. "Here you go."

Shining the flashlight in the attic, it didn't take him long to locate a small black steel box. He slid it out and handed it to Carmen, whose eyes widened as she set it on the floor. She handed him the wooden attic door and he slid it back into place. She took his hand as he stepped down from the chair.

"Follow me," she said, leading him into a room at the end of the hallway.

The room itself was a shock to Oliver, never mind what might be inside the little black box. The walls were drab with faded floral wallpaper, peeling in spots and revealing plaster. A black blind-covered window in the corner was obscured partially by a dresser. On the dresser, dozens of China dolls propped in various stages of repose, stared at them as they entered, beady eyes picking up glazed yellow reflections from the single, dangling incandescent light bulb. In the middle of the floor was a circular throw rug, woven with contrasting black and white strips. In the middle of the carpet stood a small wooden circular table. On the fringes of the rug, two worn brown leather armchairs sat facing one another. The ceiling was cracked in spots and a few pieces of plaster dangled hazardously above the table and chairs.

Another mirrored vanity furnished the opposite corner, ornamented with a few glass doll figurines, mostly ballerinas, and a small decorative jewelry box. Carmen went to the oak vanity, pulled open a drawer, and withdrew a surprisingly clean-looking white towel. She walked over to the table, dusted it off, and set the black box down. Then she dusted off the armchairs. Small plumes of dust ballooned out and settled on the black and white carpet. When she'd finished, she placed the towel on the mirrored vanity, sat in an armchair, and gestured for Oliver to follow suit.

He did. "What is this room, anyway?"

"It's not my room," she said. "If that's what you're thinking. It's Mom's room. It used to be off-limits to us, but not anymore. Mom used to come here to... I dunno... meditate, I guess."

"Looks more like she was contacting spirits," Oliver said, as Carmen twisted the key to the box.

Click!

She studied Oliver with soulful eyes. "You ready for this?"

He shuddered, suddenly feeling cold and damp. "I guess so. Do we have a choice?"

"I don't think so."

She opened the box, removed a small black book, and set it on the table. Then she removed the talisman doll and stood it on the table.

They both examined it.

Standing about a foot tall, the doll had curly brown hair, an olive complexion, large beady black eyes, and an ear-to-ear mischievous grin. Her buxom body was draped in a fluffy white dress dotted with faded red roses. Red knee-length socks and simple black slip-on shoes accessorized the turn-of-the-century ensemble.

Carmen flipped open the book and began reading.

Oliver's nerves were taut violin strings, ready to snap at the first chord. He couldn't believe the nascent yet noticeable resemblance the doll bore to Carmen. "Have you ever seen this doll before?"

"No... hang on, I'm trying to decipher these words." She removed her gaze from the book and looked at him. "Why do you ask?"

"It... *she* looks like you."

Carmen's brown eyes darkened, blackening like the doll's. "I've never seen this doll before. I found out about her when you did. I only gained access to this room a few years ago when

Mom became disabled. I hope you're not suggesting I have any nefarious intentions..."

"Forget it," Oliver said, unprepared to open this can of worms at this juncture, too afraid of what fury it might unleash. "Let's move on with the ceremony. What does the book say?"

Carmen reached into the steel box and brought out three candles, all in antique glass candle holders. She set them on the table in a semi-circle around the doll.

"We need these, according to the book," she said. "Got a light?"

"No."

Carmen rummaged around in the box and pulled out a box of matches. She half-smiled. "It looks like Mom thought of everything."

She slid the box toward Oliver and he took his cue, removing a single wooden match, lighting it, and lighting all of the candles.

He stood. "You want the light turned off?"

"I think so."

He flicked the wall switch and sat down.

The dancing candle flames cast black shadows over the doll's grinning face. A black body double behind her floated up the wall and her giant-sized head appeared in the middle of the ceiling, bobbing and weaving above them menacingly.

An ice-cold spear of fear raked up Oliver's spine as Carmen flipped pages.

She stopped at a page and placed the leather-bound book on the table, pointing to a passage.

"Right here," she said. "How to exorcise evil spirits."

"What do we do now?" Oliver said, his voice shaky.

"We join hands and I do the incantation. Put both of your hands on the table, palms up."

Oliver complied and Carmen placed both of her hands in his.

"She's Isabella," Carmen said. "That's what we have to call her from now on."

"I'll call her whatever she wants as long as she gets rid of Selina... I mean Stella."

"Okay, quiet. Let me do the incantation."

"Okay."

Carmen clasped Oliver's hands tighter, closed her eyes, and commenced humming.

"Mmmmm...   mmmmmmm... mmmmmmmmmmmmmmmmmmmmmm."

Then she opened her eyes and said, "I beseech you, oh God Almighty, to rid the presence of evil spirit—in this case, Stella—from our lives. All powerful one, I beg you to return her to the bowels of hell from whence she came..."

Oliver watched Isabella's shadow head bob and weave erratically and he thought he felt a cold gust of wind. The momentary flickering candle flames confirmed that was exactly what he had felt.

Carmen continued, "And if Stella is a part of an otherworldly struggle between good and evil, and trying to possess another spirit while possessing us, then, then... powers that be, God Almighty, I beg you to command the forces of good win out over the forces of evil..."

Oliver heard a high-pitched scream, followed by cackling laughter, and then a tornado entered the room, gained force and momentum, and circled above the table, lowering and spinning more ferociously as it descended.

He released Carmen's hands and shielded his face, watching in horror as she did the same.

The force of the mini-tornado swept up two candles, the black book, and the black box, and smashed them into the wall.

Illuminated by one mysteriously untouched candle, the Isabella doll remained where she was, her head sweeping to and fro, from Oliver to Carmen, Carmen to Oliver. Her grin widened and her eyes darkened.

Oliver quickly dove on Carmen, knocking her out of the armchair and landing on top of her, shielding her from danger with both hands as the tornado whipped and whistled ferociously around the room.

It spun violently toward the window and shattered it mercilessly. Shards of glass and the black blinds flew outside along with the last remnants of the tornado.

As the room grew quiet and still, Oliver gazed up at Isabella. She winked at him and the candle went out. Darkness enveloped the room.

He rolled off Carmen and reached for her shoulder. His hand felt something large and soft and he quickly removed it.

"Are you okay?" he asked.

"You just groped my boob."

"Sorry. I tried for your shoulder. You okay?"

"I think so."

Oliver heard a *click* and a ball of light lit up Carmen's face. It was a mask of shock yet paradoxically composed, if it were even possible for the two expressions to exist simultaneously.

"Oh… you got the flashlight," Oliver said, in between deep breaths. "Fuck… that scared the hell outta me."

"I don't think we got her," Carmen said, standing and inspecting her extremities with the flashlight. She helped Oliver up and gave him the once-over with the flashlight.

"You look okay," she said. "I mean uninjured. You okay?"

"I think so."

"Thanks, by the way."

"For what?"

For protecting me like that. That was a real act of bravery on your part. Diving on me. You even got a little grope in…"

"I didn't mean that."

Carmen ignored the comment and approached the window. She looked down at the broken glass littering the front lawn and sidewalk below, glittering in the whitewash of street lights.

Carmen groaned and turned to Oliver. "As I said, I don't think we got her."

"Who?"

"Stella. Who else?"

While Carmen picked up pieces of the mysterious puzzle, Oliver turned on the light and examined Isabella. She stared eerily into his eyes.

"Wow," Oliver said, remembering Isabella's wink but not sure whether he should disclose it. "The doll, I mean Isabella, didn't even move."

"I noticed that," Carmen said. She was crouched down with her back to him, picking up the spilled contents of the black box and collecting the black book. She put a few items inside the box, closed it, and put it on the table next to the book. She then picked up the downed candles and put them on the table. Next, she examined both the mirrored vanity and the dresser.

Oliver followed her gaze with widening eyes. None of the dolls on the dresser nor the figurines on the mirrored vanity had been touched by the furious tornado.

"Oh my God," Carmen exclaimed. "All of Mom's dolls are still in perfect condition."

"What about your Mom?" Oliver said, fearing they had just unleashed a demon, the exact opposite of what they had intended to do. *Play with fire, you'll get burned.*

"Oh, Mom could sleep through a bomb blast," Carmen said nonchalantly. "But I'll go check on her."

Oliver was at the window now, inspecting the glass-strewn lawn and sidewalk below. He glanced around at the other turn-of-the-century homes lining the street. He couldn't see a single soul, either through lit windows or on the streets below. It was as if this supernatural event had been confined to just the two of them. *Well, more than two but you know what I mean.* Several questions flashed through his mind but he shut them down through a succession of rapid eye blinks, bringing himself back into the moment.

"Do you have a dustpan and broom and garbage can? I'll clean up the glass."

Carmen went to the door and opened it. "In a closet by the front door. There's a steel garbage can at the side of the house you can use. It's empty I think."

"Okay."

Oliver followed Carmen down the stairs. Halfway down, he said, "What about that open window?"

"There's a shed out back. Plywood, hammer, and nails."

"Okay."

As Carmen entered her mother's bedroom, Oliver collected the broom and dustpan from the coat closet and stepped outside, sighing with relief as a gentle warm breeze greeted him. He went around to the side of the house, found the steel garbage can, placed it on the sidewalk, and began picking up the larger pieces of glass. His mind was only half on the task at hand, the shock of the bizarre event and the accompanying surge of adrenaline only now beginning to dissipate.

Then the floodgates opened and the questions hit him like a million waves.

What's with those dolls? Why was Isabella untouched? Have we unleashed a demon? What did Sarah's mom do with those dolls? Is she evil? Does she have an agenda? Where are the dolls from? What power do they wield? Did they bring Stella into the real world? Will she now become a part of my life and not a part of my dreams?

His mind stopped as it arrived at perhaps the two most disturbing questions. *How much does Carmen really know about the dolls? Does she have an evil agenda?*

Chapter Nine

As she sat next to her sleeping mother, troubling thoughts assaulted Carmen's mind. There seemed to be some childhood familiarity with, not only the dolls, but more particularly Isabella. Had she seen her before in spite of what she'd assured Oliver? A vague recollection of Isabella's face formed in her mind but then shattered into a million shiny pieces before it could solidify into something comprehensible.

And that room, had it really been only a few years ago that she'd gained access to it, as she'd assured Oliver? Or had she been inside it as a child? Again an indiscernible image floated and fragmented.

Her mother opened her eyes and looked at her daughter. There was a hint of fear in those eyes that Carmen hadn't noticed earlier. Previously, her mother's tone had been imperious when she'd laid out instructions to her daughter to exorcize the demon. But they hadn't exorcized anyone of anything, had they? Or maybe they had. Maybe the tornado had flushed the evil spirit, or demon, or whatever it was, out of Oliver and Carmen and blasted it, along with black blinds and shattered glass, right out of the house.

But on an instinctive level, Carmen didn't truly believe that. She was terrified on some level that they had set in motion a chain of events that would have disastrous consequences. And the person who knew for sure searched her eyes.

And finally, Sarah spoke. "What happened, my dear? You don't look like yourself."

Well, her mother had that much right. She didn't feel like herself. And now she feared, she never would.

"Something happened, Mom."

Sarah spoke slowly and deliberately. "I know that, dear. What? What happened?"

Carmen relayed the entire story, even explaining how she'd remained somewhat calm during the entire ordeal in spite of Oliver's terror. Finishing the account, Carmen said, "He's outside now, cleaning up the glass. And then he's gonna help me fix the window."

Sarah sighed. "Perhaps he's a better man than I first gave him credit for."

Something is wrong, Carmen thought. They shouldn't be discussing Oliver at a time like this. Or should they? Hadn't he caused all this? Carmen didn't know anymore and the more she thought about it the more confused she was becoming. What had happened and what was its significance? Fighting through the fog, she realized that to get that information she had to ask specific questions.

"You wanna know what this means," Sarah said evenly, evidently not needing a specific question to provide a specific answer.

"Yes, Mom. Have we unleashed a demon? Are we now free from danger? Or is this just the tip of the iceberg?"

"Were you happy to see Isabella again?"

"What?" Those same fragmented memories, pouring in like tiny pieces of a macabre jigsaw puzzle, floating loosely but failing to interlock. "I've never seen Isabella before, Mom. That was the first time."

"Of course it was, my dear. What was I thinking?"

"Did we wake you? Did the ordeal wake you?"

"No. I can sleep through a bomb blast."

"What happened, Mom? Do you have a sense of what happened?" There were other questions that came to mind, like where did she get Isabella and what did she use her for? But she couldn't let herself get distracted again. One question at a time.

Sarah closed her eyes and Carmen watched her in silence for a moment. When she opened them, several lines crinkled her brow. "I need time to think, but I don't think this is good. The last time Isabella expelled an evil spirit, there was no tornado and no broken windows. But the room shook, the house shook, and after she expelled the evil force a white calming light descended on me and on my little room. Did you feel that?"

"No."

"But you weren't scared?"

"Maybe a little. But not much." *What evil spirits has she expelled from this house? So much I don't know. Not now. Focus.* "What should we do? Oliver and me."

"Help him repair the window."

"Mom. What else? Please."

"There's nothing much you can do, my dear. Maybe you did expel the evil spirit. Maybe it's gone for good. I'll know soon enough whether I feel an evil presence in the house. I can tell you, I don't right now."

Knock... knock.

"Who is it?" Carmen said.

Oliver's voice. "I've got some plywood and some nails but I might need a hand."

Carmen opened the door and Oliver stood leaning against the door frame, a piece of plywood in one hand, a small steel toolbox in the other. "Hello."

Sarah smiled. "You gonna fix my window?"

"I'm no handyman but I'll do my best."

"Thank you."

Carmen returned to the bed, kissed her mother on the forehead, and said, "Mom, we need to talk about some stuff later."

Sarah yawned. "Tomorrow. I'm awfully drained right now."

Carmen went to the door as Oliver turned and went up the stairs.

Carmen turned around at the door. "What should I do with Isabella?"

Sarah's eyes widened. "Get reacquainted with her. Put her in your room."

Reacquainted? My room? What the hell is she talking about? Confused all over again, she turned around and followed Oliver up the stairs.

Chapter Ten

The first thing Oliver did after he'd returned home from work that Tuesday afternoon was call Carmen. They'd agreed after he'd repaired the window and left that they'd keep in touch, if only to assure themselves that they had expelled an evil spirit or demon and indeed were out of danger.

Carmen picked up on the second ring and Oliver skipped the formalities. "How was your night?"

"Uneventful. Yours?"

"The same. What about your day at work today?"

"Nothing happened. And yours?"

"The same."

Oliver exhaled a long sigh. The way things had been going he'd almost expected another disaster. "Have you talked to your mother?"

"A little bit."

"What did you learn?"

"Mom says she doesn't have a feeling one way or another at this point. Said she needs more time."

"Okay. What about Isabella? Did you put her in your room like your mother said?"

"No. I left her on the alter... ah, the table."

"So you really have nothing to report."

"I wish I could say that."

"What do you mean?"

"Remember how you said Isabella looks like me?"

"Yeah."

"Well, I started thinking about that after I got home from work today. My curiosity led me to the attic. You wouldn't believe what I found."

"What?"

"Two more dolls. They look like my brother and sister."

"Oh, shit. Have you told your mother?"

"Not yet. I think... I think she might be keeping something from us."

"Are you kidding?"

"I wish I was." Carmen's tone changed from calm to shrill. "Why does my mom have dolls that look like me and my brother, Mark, and my sister, Giselle?"

"I don't know."

"Can I come over, Oliver? I need to talk to someone and you're the only person I know who's intimately connected with this."

Oliver's mind clung to the word "intimately" for a few seconds before replying. His place was a mess and he'd have to be Superman to get it cleaned up in an hour. Nonetheless, he decided to be Superman for a day—at least an hour.

"Can you give me an hour? My place is a mess."

"I don't care if your place looks like a bomb just hit it."

"That's fairly accurate, but still, one hour please."

"See you in an hour."

***

In true Superman fashion, Oliver had just stuffed the last of three full green garbage bags into a hallway closet. He pushed the door closed and it got stuck on a corner of one of the bags. He pulled it open, kicked at the bag a couple of times, and pushed harder, finally hearing a satisfying click just as the buzzer on the wall sounded. Panting heavily, he raced to it and pressed TALK.

"Hello."

"It's me."

"Come on up."

Bzzzzzzzzzzzzzzzzzzzzzzzzzz.

He greeted Carmen at the door and led her into the living room, where he dusted off a corner of his couch before waving her into it.

She plopped herself down with a heavy sigh and looked around the apartment. "It doesn't look that bad."

"You should've seen it an hour ago."

"You Superman or something?"

"Something like that."

Oliver was still standing. "Can I get you something to drink?"

"Do you have something stronger than pop?"

"I've got an old bottle of Scotch in the cupboard I think. I use it to knock out colds and the flu. Doctors won't officially tell you that, but a stiff shot or two really helps with fever and scratchy throat."

"Get it," Carmen said.

Oliver did and after he returned with two stiff shots, he sat next to Carmen on the couch and raised his glass. "What do we drink to?"

She raised her glass. "To figure out what the hell is going on?"

They clinked glasses and drank and Carmen set her glass on the table, still a little dusty but nonetheless uncluttered. She scanned the apartment again before looking at Oliver directly, a crease forming on her brow.

"We've gotta figure out what's going on. I hate to say this... but I don't know how much I trust my mom anymore. I mean, those three dolls, all resembling us kids. What do you make of that?"

Oliver put his drink on the table, absently wiping a layer of dust, wiping his hand on his jeans, and then blushing.

"Don't worry about your apartment," Carmen said. "That's the last thing on my mind right now."

"Do you remember those dolls when you were a kid?" Oliver asked.

A pale shade of pink raced across Carmen's cheeks. "That's... that's where I have problems. I have a dim recollection of Isabella, but I have no idea where it's coming from. As a child, I don't really remember her... at least not completely."

"What about the other dolls?" Oliver asked.

"Nothing. I've never seen them except for today when I went snooping around in the attic."

"What did you do with them?"

"I put them in that... ritual room, or whatever you want to call it. They're next to Isabella."

"Have you told your mother about them?"

"No. I thought I'd talk to you first."

Oliver picked up his drink and took a swill. The strong taste bit into the back of his throat and he winced. He was starting to wonder why the heck he'd agreed to meet Carmen. Before her, it had just been he and Stella, or at least the hope of

Stella materializing. Now, maybe she already had materialized through some mysterious supernatural connection that he had yet to concretely draw. And if she was out in the real world, he was sure she wouldn't be all that happy, especially since he'd found a new friend, if he could go so far as to call Carmen a friend at this early stage. *But, wait a minute. Carmen turned into Stella at Finley's house. Before the dolls. Did Stella activate the dolls?* This was getting more fucked up and more baffling by the second.

"I think we need to write a few things down," Oliver said, getting up and retrieving a pen and note pad from a small desk drawer in the living room. He sat down again as Carmen eyed him expectantly, clearly hoping for some kind of a miracle that he doubted very much he could create.

Nevertheless, he wrote the name *Stella* on the note pad and started talking, opening up like he never had to anyone ever before in his life, like it was a matter of life and death.

"I honestly don't remember the first time I dreamt of Stella, but I felt she was my salvation. Long story short, I've been rather unsuccessful in past relationships and I thought she was my saving grace. As stupid as it sounds, I thought if I thought about it long enough, hoped and prayed for it long enough, willed it long enough, that I could bring her to life. My dream girl. I saw something in a horror movie once, can't remember the name of it, but at the beginning, it had some quote from someone that said loneliness and desperation, especially in dreams, brings on connections with the spirit world. Maybe my loneliness brought Stella to life, brought her from the dream world into the real world..."

"But how does that explain the dolls?"

Next to the name Stella, Oliver wrote *Isabella* and a question mark.

"I don't know, but here's a theory. Let's just say your mother is straight up. Let's say she kept the dolls around to prevent evil spirits from possessing her children. I mean, it fits in with the whole biological matriarchal urge to protect your young. She's never treated you poorly while you were growing up, has she?"

Carmen shook her head, picked up her drink, and took a long pull. This time she didn't put it down.

Oliver continued. "So here's my theory. Through my loneliness and desperation, I triggered Stella and brought her into the real world. She possessed you that night at Finley's and then her presence activated your mother's sixth sense. That's where the dolls come in. Stella, floating somewhere in the periphery, in some other realm, was angered by our retaliation and we felt her fury last night. And, think about it, that's why Isabella was untouched. She's a force to be reckoned with and Stella wasn't able to penetrate her brick wall of benevolence."

Carmen scratched her chin. "It does make some weird kind of sense. It also explains why Stella would possess me. She was jealous and wanted you all to herself. Also, Sigmund Freud wrote something about dreams being the manifestation of spiritual powers whose movements have otherwise been hampered or blocked during the day. It's in *Dream Psychology, Psychoanalysis for Beginners.*"

"Wow," Oliver said. "That's impressive." Beneath Stella, he wrote *evil*, below Isabella, he wrote *good*.

In the right hand corner of the page, he wrote *Sigmund Freud, Dream Psychology.*

"I mean, obviously, there's more to it than that," Oliver said. "According to your mother, there is some duality between Stella and... maybe Selina, the name I originally gave to her. Maybe it represents one spirit's struggle between two sides of her personality—good and evil. And, it's just a question of which one wins out."

"I think Stella won last night," Carmen said.

"Me too."

Oliver wrote the names *Selina* and *Stella* side by side. He then drew a line connecting them. Below *Stella*, he wrote *evil*, and below Selina, he wrote *good*. Below the names, he wrote *Two sides of the same person.*

"What do we do now?" Carmen said.

Oliver was a little stumped. To do nothing might invite the presence of Stella back into the picture and nobody wanted that. At one time, he thought that's all he would've wanted but now he didn't like the latest manifestations of Stella. Yet he was quite sure it wouldn't end well if they stood idly by and did nothing. *The dolls. Isabella is the antithesis of Stella and exactly what we need to repel her.*

He wrote, *More info on dolls*, and put the pen down. "We need to find out as much as we can about the dolls."

Carmen looked into her Scotch for answers. "I'm... I'm a little afraid to do that."

"Why?"

"Like I said, I have some dim recollection of Isabella but can't put a finger on it."

"You're afraid of what you might find out?"

She slowly nodded.

"Got any better ideas?"

Carmen shook her head.

"I mean, think about it," Oliver said. "Your mother believes Isabella repels evil and maybe that's why she made her, or somebody made her, in your likeness. It's to keep the evil away from you."

"Well, what about you?"

"It should work for both of us, no?"

"I don't know. What do you want me to do?"

"Find out as much as you can about Isabella and the other dolls. Bring Isabella in your room and sleep with her like you would a teddy bear if you have to. And, hey, how about this? Bring me that other one that looks like your brother Mark. I'll keep him in my bedroom to ward off the advances of Stella."

"I don't know about that," Carmen said. "I don't know if Mother would approve."

"Okay, forget about the Mark doll for now. But, why don't you go find out what you can while there's still time?"

There was another reason Oliver wanted to get rid of Carmen now, but he would never admit it to himself. The Scotch had gone to his head. The more he looked at Carmen, her voluptuous form almost bursting from her tight black jeans and body-hugging pink V-neck blouse, the more he was becoming attracted to her. He'd felt himself inching closer to her as the conversation had progressed and he realized it would be too much too soon to try and make a move. But the truth was he hadn't been laid in so long he couldn't remember, and he would like nothing better than to snuggle up with this enigmatic woman in his bed. *Too much too soon. Too much too soon.*

And Carmen seemed to take the cue. In one long gulp, she polished off her Scotch and stood. "I'm gonna go see what I can find out. Can I call you later?"

"Of course."

Chapter Eleven

Maybe it was the Scotch. Maybe it was that he just wanted to be sure about Stella's intentions. Maybe Stella had nothing to do with what had been happening lately and all of this crazy shit had been brought on by Carmen and her demons. Whatever it was, Oliver wanted to be sure.

As soon as Carmen left, he turned his cellphone off, brought another glass of Scotch into his bedroom, and put it on an end table. Then he cleared some clothes off his bed and piled them all into a laundry hamper in one corner of the bedroom. He picked up a few empty chip bags and chocolate bar wrappers, dumped them into the kitchen garbage can, returned with a broom, and swept out his entire bedroom. How could he possibly attract a woman, any woman, if he remained a fucking slob? He retrieved a small candle in a glass jar, lit it, and placed it on the nightstand.

He stretched out on the bed and watched the flickering flames dance around the ceiling, a black flower growing and shrinking, growing and shrinking.

"Is that you?" he said to an empty room. "Have you finally come for me, Stella? I need to know your intentions because, otherwise, I fear your days are numbered."

After a few moments of silence, the black flower petals quadrupled in size, encasing half the ceiling.

Oliver heard what he thought was a knock on the door.

His heart raced. "Is that you, Stella? Is that you?" One part of him knew he was playing with fire. And the other part, the part that had been attracted to and obsessed with Stella for far too long, didn't care.

The door creaked open.

Oliver gasped.

***

After she'd arrived home, Carmen had fed her mother, given her some painkillers, and let her doze for a few minutes before re-entering the room. Now she sat bedside in the candle-lit bedroom and leaned in close to Sarah. She didn't want her mother to miss a single word she had to say. But first things first.

"Mom, last night, did you get any sense of what happened? Whether ultimately it's good or bad?"

Through her hollow eye sockets, Sarah looked at her daughter, her face turning an ashen gray, and said, "Something went wrong."

A cold chill crept up Carmen's spine. "What went wrong?"

"Isabella is your protector. But last night, she wasn't able to complete her work. She expelled the evil—this demon called Stella—but not permanently. Instead of banishing her to the bowels of hell, I feel she's been unleashed into the world." Her mother's eyes widened. "She'll come for Oliver, and then she'll come for you."

"When, Mom? When?"

"You have some time, my dear. Don't panic. I guess it's time you knew."

Carmen thought she may as well come clean. "I found the other two dolls in the attic, Mom. Mark and Giselle."

Her mother did not look surprised. "I thought you might. Where are they?"

"They're all in your secret room."

"Good. For now." Sarah brushed back a strand of her gray hair, still full and thick after all these years. "Do you remember your father?"

Carmen inhaled deeply. The subject of Matheson had always been taboo while she was growing up. When she was old enough to understand, her mother had simply explained that Matheson had died in a terrible car crash when she was the tender age of two. She saw no reason to doubt it, no reason to investigate it. What was her mother hiding?

"How can I remember him, Mom? He died when I was two. In a car crash, you told us."

"That's what I said, but that wasn't the truth," Sarah said. "That's not the truth. It was just easier at the time. But now that Isabella is out of the closet, err attic, along with your brother and sister, I think you should know. No, you need to know, because I don't have long with this world, my dear, and I do not want to take this to my grave with me."

Carmen was growing worried and scared. "What happened?"

Sarah's eyes widened and a red streak flashed across her face, elongated garishly by the shadow from the flickering candle flame. "The devil took his soul. The evil got the better of him. He was a good man, although drink and gambling, the devil's poisons, infected his soul and he was taken from me. Right in this house, he was taken from me. I didn't know what to do so I started reading about the occult. Then one day I was shopping downtown and I strolled past an antique dealer. In the window was Isabella, staring at me, grinning at me, but yet offering her protection and summoning me inside. She looked so much like you, my dear, I went in and bought her, added her to my doll collection. The man in the store, he's long dead now, told me that Isabella would protect you from harm. I told him about my other children and he said he had other dolls. I returned with some photos of Mark and Giselle, and, well, you know the rest, I suppose. They're upstairs now."

Carmen didn't really know the rest and many questions popped into her head; and then a sense of guilt. She'd had a stiff shot of Scotch at Oliver's. Was that enough to summon the devil or the devil's evil minions? But there were other more pressing concerns.

"Mom, so you're saying those three dolls protect us kids from evil?"

Sarah nodded.

"And that's what you were doing in that ritual room?"

"That's right, my child. Every time I felt you or Mark or Giselle were in danger I would bring the corresponding doll in, pray, and summon God's powers to protect you. Finally, when you were out of danger, and I knew all of you were pursuing morally upright lives, I put them away."

"Why didn't you tell us?" Carmen asked, deciding against telling her mother that in her view Giselle and Mark were pretty far from morally upright. No point upsetting her mother in her golden years, if this is what they were.

"I couldn't. You'd think I was crazy. You probably already do."

"No. Not after what happened."

Sarah's eyes grew morose and she gave her daughter a knowing look. "You've had a drink tonight, haven't you?"

"I had some Scotch at Oliver's. Just a shot. And last weekend at my friend Ruby's, when I first met Oliver, I drank some wine. Will that get me in trouble?"

"I wouldn't take any chances. After what happened to your father, I never touched another drop."

Something her mother had said to her at the beginning of this conversation darted into her mind, a response to a question about how much time they have before the evil returns. *You have some time, my dear. Don't panic.*

"Mom, you said, I have some time before the evil returns. What about Oliver?"

Sarah closed her eyes and what little color she had drained from her face. She blinked many times and then opened her eyes wide. "Oliver is in immediate danger."

***

There she is. In the flesh. Oliver had gasped when she'd first entered his bedroom and now he lay in bed, wide-eyed and jaw-dropped, speechless and incredulous that his creation, his dream woman, had miraculously materialized.

And she looked just like he'd imagined she would.

She stood at the entrance to the door, backlit by a hallway light he'd forgotten to turn off. Long black hair, statuesque and curvy, and wearing a shiny black, form-hugging bodysuit. He could barely make out her high cheekbones and chiseled features in the suffused and flickering candlelight. But he had noticed that the dancing ceiling flower had vanished.

Oliver finally spoke, "Is it really you? Are you really Stella?"

She closed the door and stepped into the room, making a show of strutting her stuff around the bed. She stopped and grinned. "It's really me. And I'm really Stella."

"Are you evil?"

"What do you think? You conjured me up. Are you evil?"

"No. Maybe a little obsessive and selfish, but not evil."

Stella stopped at the foot of the bed and peeled back the shoulder straps of her bodysuit. Mammoth, gravity-defying melons popped out, spear-like erect nipples pointing directly at Oliver's head. "Then neither am I."

Oliver felt his member stiffen and he knew there was no turning back now. Everything in the past was all bullshit. This was his dream woman, finally here to consummate everything he'd been dreaming, wishing, and praying for... for oh-so many years.

He watched Stella rake a long-nailed finger down the mid-section of the bodysuit. It sprang open and withered to the floor, revealing her sensuous nakedness. In a flash, she darted forward, peeled his socks off, tore his pants off, ripped his shirt off, and jumped on him, grabbing his penis and stuffing it roughly into her.

"Oh, oh my God," Oliver said, beginning a slow and steady moaning as she pinned his arms to the mattress and began pounding ferociously.

"God?" she said. "God has nothing to do with this."

She released his arms and Oliver, in spite of her nerve-rattling declaration, cupped both of her breasts in his hands. They felt hard and cold to the touch but he didn't care, so transported was he by the ecstasy of the moment. It had been too long and he wanted to feel her flesh, wanted to explode inside her, wanted to escape this earthly realm and be with her forever, wherever she dwelled. Thoughts flashed through his mind. His own stupid theory about how his loneliness and desperation had given birth to evil spirits. His willingness to expel Stella from his life with the help of Carmen and those silly dolls. All hogwash. This was real. This was magnificent. This was now.

Then Stella gripped his throat and suddenly it was real and it was now, but it was no longer magnificent anymore. Oliver felt his neck constrict quickly and gasped for breath. He managed to squeak, "What're you doing?" before her powerful hands silenced his ability to speak. It was all he could do to gasp and squirm and fight for his life.

Stella watched her progress approvingly and finally said, "You think I'm what you want? You're a fucking pathetic loser."

Her grip tightened and Oliver felt a blackness, the darkness of death, begin to cloak him.

He heard a loud thud and the bedroom door burst open.

He felt the iron-grip of the noose around his neck loosen. Stella turned into a black misty substance, swirled around the room ferociously, and disappeared out the open bedroom door, trailed by a slow and agonizing scream.

Holding a doll in each arm, pressed against each breast, Carmen, herself cloaked in black, stood at the bedroom door, mouth and eyes wide open, a mask of fear.

Embarrassed, petrified, and panting for breath, Oliver covered his erect penis with a pillow and stared at Carmen. It took him a few seconds to stammer out the words. "How... how did you get in?"

She set the dolls on a nearby dresser and turned to Oliver. "Someone leaving your building let me in."

"What about my apartment?"

"Someone left the door open. I knocked but no one answered. Then when I heard the moaning, I rushed in."

Carmen sat down on the foot of the bed and Oliver inched away. He pulled at a blanket, quickly covering his nakedness with it but leaving the pillow in place as an extra layer of protection. The blanket-pillow combination concealed the tent pole, transforming it to a mountain, or at least a molehill.

"Thanks," Oliver said, finally finding his breath.

Carmen nodded, searching his eyes intently.

"She tried to kill me," Oliver said, rubbing his reddening neck. "Did you see her?"

"No, I only saw and felt a dark force rush past me and heard her agonizing screams. What were you doing? What *are* you doing? Did you summon her?"

Oliver was silent for a moment as Carmen searched his eyes. He averted her gaze.

"You *did*," she said. "What on God's green Earth do you think you're doing? I thought you were on my side. I mean, you're the one who told me to find out about the dolls. Told me the dolls are key to getting rid of Stella." Carmen's face flushed and she narrowed her eyes. "Why are you doing this to me?"

Oliver covered his face with both hands, trying to stem the riptide of emotion surging up inside of him. He failed dismally and tears started flowing freely down his pudgy and flushed cheeks. He choked back sobs, and said, "I'm sorry. She's all I ever wanted, all I ever dreamed about, all I ever prayed for and hoped for... for oh-so long. I guess... I guess my curiosity got the better of me and I kept trying to tell myself that Stella wasn't evil...isn't evil, and it's just a bunch of hogwash that she is...."

He trailed off, reached for a pillow, and buried his tear-stained face inside of it, trying but failing miserably to hide the muffled sobs.

Carmen looked at Oliver sternly and silently for a minute or two and waited for the sobs to abate.

Finally, he removed the pillow from his face. "I'm sorry. Will you forgive me?"

"JUST FUCKING STOP IT!" Carmen lowered her voice. "And pardon my language."

Then she leaned over and touched Oliver's neck. "Look, there are red hand prints forming on your neck. They're gonna bruise, I assure you."

In spite of the turbulent tide of emotions still swirling inside Oliver's head, he felt a tingling sensation return to his loins. The pillow mountain inched up.

Carmen saw it and looked into his eyes, a hint of lust revealed in hers.

"I'm gonna fix you," she said, peeling off the blanket, tossing the genital-covering pillow aside, and staring at Oliver's stiff and throbbing penis.

She took it in her hand and began stroking it gently.

A small moan escaped Oliver's lips.

Then she fixed him with a stern look, not missing a beat. "I don't want you to read anything into this," she said. "But if I have to redirect your sexual fantasies to put a stop to that evil bitch, then that's what I'm gonna do. Otherwise, I don't trust that you won't summon her again."

All Oliver could do was lay back and moan softly, feeling a powerful orgasm building inside of him. He surrendered to it completely.

It had been so long. So, so long.

Chapter Twelve

Carmen was all business a short time later as they sat in Oliver's living room once again, both sipping Diet Coke. She sat in an armchair across from him. He was plunked down on the couch sporting a satisfied smile.

He was enjoying the refreshing change of mood in spite of the near-death experience. *A good hand-job will go a long way to making a man's day*, he thought, conjuring up delicious images of Carmen's mammoth melons smothering his face.

She'd brought him up to speed on what she knew about the protective nature of the dolls and her mother's warning that he was in immediate danger; the reason why she'd hastily grabbed two of the dolls—the lookalike of her brother, Mark, and Isabella—and rushed to Oliver's rescue.

The dolls sat on the coffee table, Isabella facing Carmen and her brother's body-double eyeballing Oliver.

Oliver wiped a hand over his face in an effort to wipe away the satisfied smile. It didn't entirely work. He studied the male doll. It had a shock of orange hair, a bright smile, dark, round black eyes. Three strategically placed freckles dotted each cheek. It was dressed in a red-and-white button-down shirt and a pair of blue denim coveralls. A small beer belly protruded from its mid-section, reminding Oliver of his own girth.

"Does he have a name?" Oliver said. "Or is he named after your brother?"

"Mom said he's called Milton," Carmen said matter-of-factly. "And I say you should keep him."

"Does your mother agree with that opinion?"

"I didn't have a chance to ask her. It was a bit of an emergency."

"Do you think it was Milton and Isabella who got rid of Stella?"

"I know it was," Carmen said. "I just know it. If it weren't for them and me, you'd be dead."

"Thanks again for that," Oliver said, absently rubbing his neck. It stung where it had been wrung.

Carmen stood. "Do you have any cream? I should put something on that."

Oliver relished the thought of her hands on him again, even it was just his neck. "In the bathroom. Skin moisturizer."

She walked down the hall, went into the bathroom, and returned with a bottle of moisturizer. She knelt in front of him and motioned for him to lean forward. He did.

She squirted a large white blob of it on her hands, wiped them together, and started massaging Oliver's neck.

"You better stop it," he said, feeling an uncontrollable tingling sensation in his loins.

"Getting horny again?" she said as she gently worked the lotion into his neck.

"Yeah," he admitted.

"Well, I'm not giving you another hand-job. That was to keep Stella away."

How about a blow-job then? Or a good fuck session. Damn, my thoughts have never been that crass before. What did that bitch do to me?

Carmen removed her hands. "What's wrong with you? You're tensing up."

He waved a hand to the armchair. "I'm sorry. Thanks for doing that. You better sit over there. I'm getting a lot of erotic thoughts about you."

Carmen backed away and, as she sat down, Oliver thought he saw her try to hide a faint smile.

Maybe she likes this. Maybe this is all a game to her.

"I don't think you should go to work like that tomorrow," she said. "You better call in sick."

He touched his neck. He'd examined the strangle marks earlier in the mirror and had to admit it was not becoming. They were already turning purple.

"It's okay," he said. "I'll wear a light turtleneck to hide them."

"In the middle of summer? You can't go to work tomorrow. And, if you don't mind, I think I should stay here tonight." She arched her dark and well-manicured left eyebrow seductively.

"Sure," he said quickly. "You can sleep with me."

"No. I'll sleep on the couch. I want to keep an eye on you, especially after what happened."

"You don't trust me?"

"I don't trust your urges... and the influence Stella has over you."

Oliver had to admit she had a point. In a matter of hours, he'd gone from ardent enemy to staunch supporter of Stella and he wasn't sure he trusted his own impulses, even though they'd been somewhat quelled by the recent activities in the bedroom.

"This couch folds out into a bed," Oliver said, tapping a worn cushion. And I have extra blankets and a pillow in a closet. He rose, went to the closet, removed the linens, and plopped them down on the couch. Then he went to the door, secured the deadbolt and the handset lock, and sat down.

"What about the dolls?" Oliver asked.

"You take Milton into your room and I'll sleep with Isabella."

"What about your mother?"

"She should be okay for a few hours. I'll leave early."

Chapter Thirteen

Sarah opened her eyes abruptly. A cold chill had swept through the room, waking her from a deep sleep, albeit one filled with nightmares of the loss of her late husband, Matheson. Telling her daughter earlier in the evening about his untimely death-by-demon possession had opened up a horrifying can of worms, worms that for many years she'd managed to keep buried in the dirt. But she hadn't told Carmen the full story. She hadn't had time, since a clear and present danger to the well-being of Oliver had emerged and her daughter had made the decision to rush to his aid.

Sarah scanned the bedroom and saw nothing but the suffused glow of the blue nightlight plugged into a nearby wall outlet. She then focused on the images from the nightmare still lingering in her mind.

Her nightmare had been identical to the reality, she realized, recalling that painful event so many years ago. Matheson had returned home late one night from playing poker in the smoky back room of a neighborhood pool hall. He'd arrived drunk and penniless, much like he had on many other occasions.

She replayed the conversation in her mind.

"Dear, you have to stop this drinking and gambling. We have a family. We have children to raise. Where are we gonna get the money to do that if you keep blowing it?"

He stopped at the foot of the stairs and eyeballed his wife with bloodshot and sad eyes. Although he'd become addicted to two deadly and dangerous vices, he'd never laid a hand on his wife or his children, preferring instead to drown his evident sadness, discontent, and inferiority issues in the bottle and gambling.

"I'm sorry, dear," he said. "I know I've gotta stop before it's too late."

How many times had he said that? Sarah thought. His resolve would last for a week, two at best, and then he'd return to the same vices, hoping for that one big win to catapult the family out of debt and into financial and emotional well-being.

But now was not the time or place to reprimand him. Instead, she'd helped him upstairs, helped him undress, tucked him into bed, kissed him lightly on the forehead, and said, "Goodnight," offering a sliver of hope—"tomorrow is another day"—before turning out the bedside lamp and returning to bed.

She remembered being precipitously jarred to her senses by a cold draft that had rushed into the room, seemingly penetrating the bedroom door.

She felt the wind swirl around and form a powerful tornado before a black misty substance emerged and those blood-red, piercing, horrifying eyes. Then, boom, she watched, catatonic with fear, as Matheson's soul was snatched away, his vapory image disappearing through the ceiling along with the black misty substance.

She'd screamed loud, horrifying, and blood-curdling. And when she'd strained her vocal cords to the point where she could scream no more, she'd heard the defiant and resolute response.

"It's too late for him."

On the verge of screaming again, Sarah opened her eyes, remembering vividly what had happened next. When the fear-induced catatonia had thawed, she'd leaned over to her husband and checked for a pulse.

There was none.

He was dead.

The devil had snatched his soul.

Strangely, the only child who had woken up had been Carmen. She'd entered the room and, seeing her mother embracing her father, tears streaming down her face, had herself burst into tears, toddled into her bedroom, and locked her door. She'd been only two years old at the time, and to this day—*thank God*—she never remembered the incident.

A coroner's report had revealed that Matheson had died of a heart attack in his sleep and that had been the end of it. Sarah bought the dolls, concealed the truth from her children, and did the best she could to raise them to be God-fearing, scrupulous, productive members of society.

She sighed heavily. "At least I think I've accomplished that, thanks to you, my dear Lord."

A window blind fluttered and caught Sarah's eye. She gripped the blankets tightly. "No, no, you're not coming back now."

The blind swirled defiantly and a black misty apparition slowly formed. It floated into the room and up toward the ceiling. As it did, the image became more discernable—a cape-wearing woman with long black hair.

Staring wide-eyed at the image, Sarah's mouth dropped open into a wide O of horror. When she saw the blood-red eyes, she froze, catatonic.

The caped woman swirled around the room, cackling demonically.

Sarah struggled to move, struggled to speak, but to no avail. Her eyes darted back and forth as the demon descended on her. Out of the corner of her eye, she thought she saw a large, lizard-like tail form and plunge toward her open mouth. Her mind raced. *The dolls. Where is my protection? Where is Carmen? Had she taken Milton and Isabella to Oliver's in the hope of saving him? Yes, surely she had. But, wait. That left Grace, the name she'd given to the Giselle doll.*

"Oh, no, you don't," an ear-piercingly loud, high-pitched voice said, reading her mind. "Your time has come. Try to save your daughter. Try to save Oliver. NO FUCKING WAY!!!"

"Grace," Sarah shouted, feeling an unpleasant burning sensation in her chest.

The bedroom door flung open with a loud bang.

Sarah broke free from the vice-like catatonia and watched as Grace floated into the room. An angry expression had replaced her usual playful grin. Her long blonde hair was matted to her freckly face. Her dark eyes were laser-focused on the swirling black apparition. The doll's outstretched arms reached for the tail.

But, as she got to within an inch of it, Sarah heard a loud and agonizing scream and the evil black apparition dissipated in an instant. Its last malicious remnants disappeared right through the bedroom ceiling.

Grace's mission accomplished, she stopped in mid-air and dropped onto the bed. Then she nestled snugly between Sarah's shoulder and outstretched arm.

A dagger pierced Sarah's heart. She winced and groaned. Then she gasped for breath, hugged Grace, and tried to scream. All that emerged was a raspy, nasal sound.

Sarah closed her eyes and her heart stopped beating.

Chapter Fourteen

Carmen was shaking Oliver but he wasn't waking up. She'd woken up to a phone call at precisely 3:33 am on that weird Wednesday morning. Police Detective Stanley Darby had politely informed her that her mother had been rushed to the hospital after a neighbor had noticed a window smashed at her residence and had called 911. Sarah was now in the intensive care unit of the Toronto General Hospital and the cop had no idea if she was even still alive. All he could say was that Sarah had evidently had a heart attack.

Carmen tugged at Oliver's arm. "Come on, Oliver. Wake up! It's an emergency."

He stirred and finally opened his eyes. "What's wrong?"

"It's my mom. She's had a heart attack." She pulled him out of bed. "Come on. We're going to the hospital."

For a big man, Carmen thought, *Oliver sure responded quickly after hearing the tragic news*. She was already dressed and ready to rock and she watched him scramble around the room, pulling his pants on and then buttoning up a brown long-sleeved shirt he'd quickly removed from a cluttered dresser drawer. Then she realized the inappropriateness of staring at him dressing and went to the bedroom door.

"I'll wait for you in the living room."

"Okay. Make sure you bring the dolls. There's a knapsack in the hallway closet by the door."

***

Both fidgety and sipping strong but lukewarm vending machine coffees, Carmen and Oliver sat in a crowded waiting room of the Toronto General Hospital. It was adjacent to an Emergency Ward waiting room and it appeared the overflow had come to meet and greet them. A scrawny man with an unkempt mop of black hair sat next to Carmen, pressing a white towel onto a bleeding wrist. The towel was saturated with blood.

Next to Oliver, an overweight middle-aged woman sat slumped over, her head in her hands, expressing an occasional grief-stricken sob. The twenty-odd other visitors were attending to their wounds or otherwise silent, either with their grief or anxiousness. One skinny, clean-cut man in the far corner of the room occasionally coughed loudly, neglecting to cover his mouth with either his arm, his hand, or a tissue. Every time he coughed, one or two people would stand up and give him a wide berth. He coughed again and a young punk-rock themed man with a disheveled mane shot him an annoyed glance, got up, and joined the other patients standing in a queue by the waiting room door.

The punker narrowed his eyes and pointed an accusatory finger at the cougher. "Why don't you cover your mouth when you cough?"

The skinny man glared at the punker, pushed his horn-rimmed glasses up his long pointy nose, and clenched a fist. "Why don't you go fuck yourself?"

The sobber uncovered her face and narrowed her eyes at the cougher. "Hey, there's no reason to start using language like that. Why don't you watch your mouth?"

"Why don't you go fuck yourself, too?" the cougher said, ejecting spittle along with his vitriol.

Carmen and Oliver looked at one another, rolling their eyes and shaking their heads.

A young bald man wearing a white lab coat entered the room, sized up the situation instantly, and said, "Folks, please let's behave ourselves."

There was a momentary quiet. He regarded Oliver and then Carmen. "You must be Carmen Weathersby."

Carmen nodded and stood.

Oliver also stood, scratching his head and wondering how the man knew who Carmen was. They'd never met him and, after their initial inquiries, were told to wait in the waiting room for word from a doctor on Sarah's condition.

As the doctor approached, Oliver chalked it up to one of life's little mysteries and didn't give it a second thought.

"I'm Doctor Russell Stevens," the man said, not offering his hand.

"Carmen, and my friend Oliver."

"Forgive me for not shaking your hand," the doctor said, casting a sideways glance at the cougher. "I'm sure you understand."

Carmen and Oliver gave him a knowing look.

"Follow me, he said, turning around and heading for the door.

"Is it okay if my friend comes?" Carmen asked.

The doctor stopped, seemed to ponder it for a moment, but as another loud, hacking cough erupted from the cougher, he quickly made up his mind. "Okay."

They left the waiting room and followed the doctor down a hallway and into an office. The doctor opened the door, let them in, and closed it behind them, saying, "Take a seat."

They sat across from him at his desk. He gave them the once-over as if he had a bionic eye that was diagnosing their physical and mental conditions.

If only he knew, Oliver thought.

He opened a file on his desk and studied it.

"How is she?" Carmen said.

"Your mother is lucky to be alive," Doctor Stevens said. "At her age, she's extremely fortunate paramedics got to her when they did. They were able to resuscitate her en route to the hospital."

"Can we see her now?" Carmen said with a loud sigh.

"I'm afraid not," Doctor Stevens said. "Your mother slipped into a coma. My team is still with her in the Intensive Care Unit, trying to stabilize her."

"A coma?" Carmen said. "Oh my God, no."

"I'm afraid so," the doctor said, scribbling something in the file. "I have to be straight with you. At her age, it's unlikely she'll come out of it. Soon, you might have some difficult decisions to make."

Oliver knew where this was going and he could see by Carmen's pained expression, she did as well. *Pulling the plug. Almost a form of euthanasia.*

"But don't think about that now," Doctor Stevens said. "Let's hope, by the grace of God, Sarah *does* pull through. And, if she does, I would suggest to you that a nursing home is probably the best place for her."

"I've realized that for some time," Carmen said. "I just wanted to respect my mom's wishes and care for her by myself for as long as I could."

"Well, I think that time has come."

With that, the doctor wrote down Carmen's contact details, handed her a business card, and instructed her to inquire later today or tomorrow regarding Sarah's condition and a possible visit. After that, he ushered them out the door. As he closed it behind them, he arched an eyebrow and said, "Pray for her. Pray for your mother."

***

Before leaving the hospital, Carmen and Oliver had called in sick to their respective employers. They'd decided to drive straight to Carmen's house, repair the window damage, and examine Sarah's bedroom for clues as to why she suddenly had a heart attack in the middle of the night. It was 5:36 am and the streets were clogged with morning work commuters. Finally, Oliver pulled down the inner-city residential street where Carmen lived, located the old brick two-story home, and parked in front of it. The morning sun was just coming up over a wall of skyscrapers in the distance.

He reached into the back seat but then noticed Carmen already had the green knapsack, hugging it firmly against her bosom.

"Are they in there?" Oliver asked.

She nodded. "They're okay."

"Bring them inside."

"Oh, don't worry, I will."

Given the circumstances, Oliver imagined he and Carmen must continue traveling with their respective dolls, carrying them around in knapsacks everywhere they went. The concept seemed ludicrous on one hand, absolutely necessary on the other.

Inside Sarah's bedroom, Carmen's mouth dropped open when she saw the Grace doll, the body-double of her sister Giselle, lying on the bed, flat on her back, smiling up at them.

"She's Grace," Carmen explained. "The doll for my sister."

"What's she doing on your mother's bed? I thought you left her in that ritual room."

"I did," Carmen said, picking up the doll and gently stroking her hair.

"Well then, how did she get here? I'm sure the paramedics or the cops would have no reason to bring her down."

Carmen fixed Oliver with a somber gaze. "I think you know how she got here. I think we both do."

Oliver removed his black baseball cap, an impromptu bed-hair protector, scratched his head, and replaced it. "Grace tried to rescue your mother from Stella."

Carmen nodded slowly, gently placed Grace between the disheveled sheets, and slid a pillow under her smiling face. She admired her work briefly and then turned to Oliver. "I think we should get Grace to the hospital as soon as possible. Mom might need her."

Oliver nodded and then approached the shattered window. Most of the glass had been thrust outward, sucking the window coverings with it. Oliver stepped carefully around a few shards of glass. "I'll clean this up. You got some gloves and a broom and dustpan?"

"I think they are where you left them."

"In the closet by the door?"

Carmen nodded, checking the time on the bedside digital clock: 6:36 am. "I think I'm gonna call a glass guy to replace both windows. No point boarding everything up. The place will look abandoned and haunted."

"Good idea," Oliver said, thinking the home already looked haunted. *Never mind looked, it is haunted.*

Oliver left the room and returned gloved and holding a broom and dustpan. He swept up glass bits and then stopped, raising both eyebrows as a series of creases snaked across his forehead. "What about your sister and brother?"

Carmen had removed Isabella and Milton from the knapsack and was tucking them in alongside Grace in Sarah's bed.

Oliver watched her, beginning to think this whole business was turning into a scene from one of his B-grade horror flicks. The only problem was, you could laugh at them. He found nothing at all funny as he watched Carmen care for the dolls. On the contrary, it was becoming more and more terrifying by the day.

"Oh, shit," Carmen said, placing Milton's hand on Isabella's shoulder. "I forgot all about them in my panic. I wonder if the cops called them."

"Dunno," Oliver said. "I wonder how the cops got your number so fast."

"I had a business card here on Mom's bedside table. There's a pay-as-you-go cellphone in the drawer here in case of emergencies. The card's gone. The cops must've put two and two together."

"Anyway, you better call your brother and sister. Don't you think?"

"I will," Carmen said. "Frankly, they don't really give a shit about Mom, but you're right, I should warn them."

"Not to mention that now that we know Stella has been unleashed they might be in danger," Oliver said. "And they don't have the dolls for protection—like we do."

Carmen pulled her cellphone from her pants pocket, frowned, set it on the bedside table, and sat on the bed next to the dolls. She looked at the dolls, at Oliver, the dolls, and finally back to Oliver.

"And just how do I explain that to them? You want me to take Milton away from you?"

"No," Oliver said. "Especially now, we need to take these dolls with us everywhere we go."

"I agree," Carmen said. She regarded her cellphone as if it had sprouted fangs. "Maybe I won't mention the dolls."

"I'll leave that up to you," Oliver said, emptying a glass-filled dustpan into a nearby wastebasket. "And, if you decide in the end that Mark is more deserving than I am to have Milton, then I guess there's nothing I can do about it. I'll go along with it I guess."

Carmen went to the door. Opening it, she spun around and faced Oliver. "Don't worry," she said with a half-smile. "I'll tell them about Mom but won't mention the dolls."

"You might also want to tell them to watch their backs," Oliver said.

But Carmen had already left, closing the door tightly behind her.

***

She went into the living room, sat down, stared at the phone, and thought about how she would word this. She'd barely spoken to Mark or Giselle in the last year. But there had been two phone calls. One from Mark, inquiring nonchalantly about Sarah's condition. And there was a long and telling silence on the other end of the line when Carmen had said, "She's doing well. Even gained five pounds in the last month."

She knew Mark enough to know what he wanted—his share of Sarah's estate, mostly tied up in the Toronto inner-city home, now worth well over a million dollars.

And there wasn't a lot of daylight between Mark and Giselle. The last time Giselle had called, she'd asked about Power of Attorney, wanting to get her greedy hands on Sarah's bank account so she could decide what her mother wanted and when she wanted it.

But that wasn't gonna happen, Carmen knew. In the will, she had Power of Attorney and the POA also specified that should her mother become mentally incapable of making decisions, then Carmen could invoke the POA immediately.

Fucking heartless, money-grubbing losers.

She opened her phone, found her brother in the contact list, and lowered her trembling finger to the speed-dial CALL button. But her finger stopped a millimeter before pressing it.

Screw them. I'll call them tonight after Oliver leaves.

Chapter Fifteen

She opened her eyes and realized that although the last few days had been mostly a blur, she had accomplished some things. The last time she'd put her mind to it, she'd kicked the shit out of that other evil woman, saved herself from the sinkhole, and sent that malicious bitch plummeting into it.

And she'd accomplished something else as well. After that life-and-death battle with the evil woman, she'd vowed to dedicate herself to discovering who she really was, or who she really had been.

And she'd gone some way to doing that. She knew now she wasn't Stella. Stella was evil. She was good. She was Selina. How she knew that, she didn't know. But she knew it to be true.

A snapping sound followed by a flash of pain across her naked breasts snapped her back into her grim reality.

"Oww," she shouted, struggling to move. But the clink of metal around her wrists and ankles quickly informed her that she was being held captive. For the first time, she noticed her surroundings. A dungeon-like, rock-walled, dimly lit room. She raised her head and looked up.

In front of her stood the blackly clad woman, grinning and holding a whip. She was backlit by a subtle yellow glow, which mysteriously accentuated her maniacal expression.

"You think you've figured everything out," the whip-woman said. "Stella and Selina. Don't you know what's really going on?"

"You're Stella and I'm Selina. I had it all wrong."

The woman curled the whip around her arm, preparing for another strike. "I'll grant you that. I'm Stella and you're Selina, but do you know who we really are?"

"You're evil and I'm good."

"You've got that right," Stella said. "But you're still lukewarm."

Selina was becoming confused. First, she was Stella, now Selina. But who was she really? A horrifying possibility began to dawn on her. But, no, it couldn't be. She refused to give it voice.

Stella cracked the whip again and the tip of it caught Selina above the right eye. A two-inch gash opened up and blood dribbled into Selina's eye, down her nose, and into her mouth.

She screamed from the physical pain and from a new and grim realization of what she believed was really going on.

Stella curled the whip around her arm and grinned. "You're getting warmer, sunshine. Give up?"

"No, no."

"What does that mean?" Stella asked. "You give up or you don't wanna hear what I have to say?"

Selina licked her lips and spit a mouthful of blood onto the cold, hard concrete floor. "Fuck you."

Stella cracked the whip again and Selina felt another flash of pain as the metal tip sliced across her stomach, opening up a wide gash and producing more blood.

Selina bit her tongue, determined not to show weakness.

"Alright, I'll tell you," Stella said, placing the whip on a nearby table cluttered with other instruments of torture. "We are one and the same. Two sides of the same being struggling for domination. A colossal battle between the forces of good and evil. Last time you won. This time I win. And, as long as I keep you chained up, I'll continue to win."

Selina spit another glob of blood on the floor. She would have targeted Stella, but Stella was standing just out of range. *Besides, she's me. Should I spit at myself? Yeah, she's whipping you, isn't she?*

"Oh, don't worry," Stella said, reaching for a black chair that appeared out of nowhere and sitting down. "I can't hurt you that much. That would be hurting myself. I just wanted to show you that I'm the boss. As long as I keep you in chains, I can do whatever the fuck I want. I can flourish. Evil, the true nature of the human species, can flourish."

"You won't get away with this," Selina said. "I'll... I'll stop you."

Stella rose from the chair and strutted forward, the tight black bodysuit accentuating her perfectly proportioned curves. She stopped within three feet of Selina. "How you gonna do that?"

"I'll... I'll find a way," Selina stammered, rattled by the recent revelation. *She's me. My God, how did this happen? Who did this?*

"Why, the higher power did this," Stella said, moving in closer, reading her alter-ego's mind. "And I'll tell you one thing; he's not who everyone thinks he is."

It was time for the question that had been haunting Selina for what seemed like generations. "What are we? Are we alive? Are we human?"

Stella bent down and licked the line of blood dripping from Selina's mid-section.

Selina cringed and shivered. "Stop that."

Stella locked eyes with her. "Oh, but you'll like it, my dear. It's masturbation to be sure, but on a much grander and much more satisfying scale."

Selina struggled futilely as she watched Stella glide her tongue along the trail of blood and lick it up with a loud slurping sound. As Stella devoured the oozing blood, the six-inch gash across Selina's stomach magically healed.

Stella stopped and winked at Selina. "Don't be afraid. See, I'm healing you."

Selina had no answer for that. She stopped squirming, it was pointless anyway, and watched Stella's ravenous tongue slither up toward her ample breasts. As she licked across one mound, Selina noticed the red welt left by the whip start to fade to an olive tone, like the rest of her supple skin.

Stella stopped and grinned at Selina. "See, I'm the great healer. Look at me as your immune system on steroids."

Leaving a three-inch red welt that circled Selina's protruding nipple and areola, Stella moved up to Selina's face, kissing her tenderly on the cheek before tonguing the small cut above her right eye and then licking it clean of blood. Stella then circled Selina's eye with her serpent-like tongue, slurped up the remaining blood on her dainty nose, and then began licking Selina's lips clean.

Selina closed her mouth, held her breath, not knowing whether to scream or moan. Her wounds were being magically healed. How could she fight it?

Stella grinned. "You're enjoying this," she said, planting a wet kiss on Selina's lips before her probing tongue found the injured breast. Her tongue licked the red welt and it vanished.

Stella quickly moved to the rock-hard nipple, sucking it deep into her mouth and then licking it tenderly.

Selina winced, wanting desperately to scream. But when she finally did open her mouth, all that escaped was a soft moan.

Chapter Sixteen

Mark Weathersby hung up the phone in the hallway of his house, ending the call with his sister Carmen at 9:36 pm that Wednesday evening.

A mischievous smile illuminated his thin face. He'd been feeding his girlfriend—now common-law wife since she'd moved in with him six months ago—a line of bullshit for the last year, telling her he was a big player in the Toronto real estate development game and on the verge of a big payday. In actuality, he was in debt up to his eyeballs and on the verge of declaring bankruptcy. He managed his money about as well as a newborn baby manages a game of chess.

And now, with the news that her mother was in the hospital in a coma, it looked likely that he was on the threshold of a big payday. At her age, surely Sarah couldn't last much longer. And Mark knew only too well that all her children had been provided for equally in the will.

He scrolled to the calculator app on his smartphone. He had the number memorized by now, but he just wanted to see it again in black and white. His childhood home, he knew, was worth $1.7 million according to the last real estate market evaluation he'd commissioned. Since the house was a neglected wreck, that was just land value.

He quickly did the math on the calculator, dividing $1.7 million by three. $566,666.66.

As he strolled down the hallway of his rented two-bedroom suburban apartment toward the living room, he frowned slightly, realizing for the first time he'd left out real estate commissions, burial costs, legal costs, potential income tax payable, and even legal bills to probate the will and convey the title of the home to the new owner.

Never mind, he assured himself, entering the living room. *I'm still gonna be left with well over half a million.* He made a mental note-to-self to calculate these extra costs first thing tomorrow morning.

Not tonight, though. Tonight was celebration time.

His blonde-haired girlfriend, Patricia Stanton, muted the TV when Mark sat down on an armchair across from her, stopped stuffing her face with Cheetos, and wiped her orange-covered chin. She had the body of an anemic or bulimic runway model, even though she ate like a pig.

But Mark cared not about her eating habits, lack of table manners, or rough edges. He worshipped her teeny-tiny, perky tits and boney little ass. If she ever lost those attributes, he'd lose her like yesterday's trash.

"Who were you talking to?" she asked matter-of-factly. "And why do you look like you just shit in someone's corn flakes?"

"That was my mortgage broker," Mark said, knowing it wouldn't dawn on dim-witted Patricia that a mortgage broker would likely call with this kind of news during banking hours.

"What did he want at this time of the night?"

Or maybe it would dawn on her. Maybe he'd underestimated her. But it was too late now. He was already too far into the cobweb of lies and deceit. And besides, he could hardly contain his excitement. He leaped out of the armchair and threw his arms in the air, palms open, worshiping the higher powers, embracing the heavens.

"I got the money, baby. The funding came through. I've been approved for a half a million bucks."

That did get Patricia's attention. Her green eyes lit up and she quickly grabbed the remote and killed the TV, brushing a few Cheetos from her white T-shirt, sliding the half-full bowl onto the cluttered coffee table, and springing up from the couch.

She leaped into his arms and Mark shouted with glee, spinning Patricia around the room as she kissed him multiple times all over his stubbled face.

He felt her thimble-sized, rock-hard nipples pressing against his chest and sighed, knowing he was in for one hell of a fuck-fest after a few celebratory glasses of champagne.

***

Reclining in bed an hour or so later, Mark watched small red and white beads of light flash across the ceiling as vehicles six floors below passed. He'd just completed a satisfying fuck-fest with Patricia and she had her back to him now, her bony ass curled in the crook of his leg.

He was planning his day tomorrow. First things first, calculate the costs of selling the home, probating the will, etc. Then he would visit the hospital and see how his mother was doing. With any luck, she'd still be in a coma and doctors would be discussing pulling the plug on her life support and putting her out of her misery once and for all. If not, hell, maybe he'd pull the plug. He was that desperate.

A flicker of movement caught his eye and he saw the Venetian blinds sway in what appeared to be an incoming breeze. Strange. He thought he'd closed the window earlier. He climbed out of bed, found his underwear, and pulled them on.

Patricia grunted and rolled over. "What're you doing?"

Mark approached the window. "Just closing the window."

"I thought it *was* closed."

He ignored her, yanked up the window covering cord, and felt for the glass. Sure enough, the window was closed. He had remembered correctly. He *had* closed it earlier. He was about to return to bed when something caught his eye. A black misty ball, swirling mightily as it hurled through the night sky toward him.

Move, move, Mark told himself with rising panic. But he couldn't. His feet felt like they were glued to the floor.

The black ball grew in size and swirling intensity and Mark watched, horrified, as it blasted toward him.

"Come back to bed," Patricia said. "What're you staring at?"

But it was too late. The tornadic ball of fury crashed into the window, smashing it into a million pieces, crashing into Mark and sending him flying clear across the room.

He hit the wall hard and slithered down it, landing on his ass in total shock as the ball spun thunderously around the room, whipping glass and debris everywhere.

Patricia bolted up in bed. "Aaaaaaaaaaaaaaaaaaaaaaaaaaeeeeeeeeeeee!"

Two glass spears exited the spinning mass of destruction and flew toward her, one six-inch projectile penetrating her eye while the other one entered her head through her ear. She screamed again as blood sprayed like a fountain around the room.

The black ball spun itself toward Mark, flew above him for a second, and then descended rapidly. It picked him up, whirled him viciously around the room for a few seconds, and thrust him out the window.

All he had time to say was, "No, pleeeeeeeease, no!"

***

Some base survival instinct—the chicken with its head cut off—kicked in for Patricia and she scrambled out of bed. She staggered over to the window, her eye and ear raining blood droplets. The bedroom had calmed down now and the whipping debris had settled on the floor and furniture.

Patricia, dizzy from blood loss and brain damage, leaned out the window and watched Mark spiral end-over-end in mid-air. He was carried over a busy intersection and then the black ball released him and, as he plummeted to his death, the lethal black mass shot up high into the sky and vanished completely.

Patricia reached out the window and gasped. "Mark, no. Come back."

A wave of dizziness swept over her and she slumped over, impaling herself on protruding glass spears on the window ledge.

As she took her last gasping breath, the only thought that entered her troubled mind was, *Why me?*

Chapter Seventeen

A rush of chilly air awoke Giselle Weathersby at five minutes to midnight Wednesday evening. She looked around the diffusely lit bedroom of her suburban house trying to determine its source.

The room was calm, still, and dark. Yet she climbed out of bed, flicked on a bedside lamp, and thought of calling her husband, Eric. But, no, it was too late for that. A traveling wholesale vitamin salesman, he was in Vancouver on a business trip. He was due back on Saturday so she still had a few days of lonely solitude and isolation ahead of her. If he dared say, for the third time in so many months, that work, unfortunately, would delay his return trip, there would be hell to pay.

Well, maybe not hell to pay but certainly some probing questions. For the last few months, Giselle had suspected that her husband was cheating on her. And only a week ago, she'd smelled some fragrant aroma that was certainly not his cologne or her perfume on the collar of one of his shirts while she was doing laundry. She'd become so angry and obsessed at the unidentified odor that she'd shown the shirt to a Shopper's Drug Mart cosmetician and asked her to identify it.

After initially refusing, Giselle discreetly slid a fifty-dollar bill over the counter and the young woman's face brightened, immediately bringing her nose to the white shirt and saying conclusively it was Chanel No. 5.

"I fucking thought so," Giselle had said, storming out of the store in tears. It was not one of her brands. She'd fumed and fretted about it for days and, finally, in the interest of preserving her precarious relationship, swept it under the rug like she'd done in the past with so many of her other problems.

She put on a sheer, frilly white nightgown, and made her way downstairs. She went into the kitchen, flicked on a light, went to the fridge, and pulled out a carton of milk. She poured herself a glass. Hot, cold, or warm, milk always helped her sleep.

As she sipped the milk, rage boiled up inside of her. She knew. Eric was cheating. Why? At 43, Giselle had largely kept her girl-next-door good looks. Sure, she'd gained a few pounds, in all the wrong places if she had to be honest with herself, but she knew men still found her attractive. She saw the ogling eyes at the supermarket. One day, when she'd forgotten her wedding ring, a man had even approached her and asked her out. Of course, she'd politely declined, telling the tall, dark, and handsome stranger, "Thanks, but I'm married."

He'd scratched his chin, smiled, and said, "I guess if you were happily married you would've said so," before adding, "Most married women wear wedding rings."

Fucking asshole, Giselle thought, reliving his pick-up attempt over in her mind. *What had he said his name was again?* She frowned. *That's right, Lance.*

Well, he'd lived up to his name all right. He'd lanced her heart, making her painfully aware of the fragility of her marriage and the precariousness of the trust she had in her husband.

But, no she decided. There was no precariousness to the trust. It had already been shattered. That being painfully realized, Giselle began to hatch a plot. She'd always felt that because of bad decisions, she was living a life that was far beneath the life that she was meant to lead. A happy life. A happy husband. At least three children. Yet, every time she'd brought up children with Eric he'd always managed to push the subject away, saying, "There's a time and a place for everything. And we're not ready now, financially or otherwise."

Maybe he was right on the financial part, Giselle thought. He was the breadwinner. She'd refused to get a job after graduating from university with a degree in literature. Where the hell did that get you in this day and age? But it was more than that, Giselle had to admit to herself, staring vacantly around the kitchen. She had entitlement issues. She'd wanted nothing more than to be an attractive trophy wife with a happy husband and three happy and healthy children, but her biological clock was already telling her, sure kids were still possible, but certainly well past their due date.

Yet it wasn't too late. There was still hope. Her sister, Carmen, had called earlier with that hope. Mom was in a coma, probably on her death bed. She stood to be a half-million dollars in the black very soon. During an earlier phone call with her husband, she'd decided to keep that news from him. She vowed now to continue doing so for as long as possible.

Things were beginning to come clear. She'd collect her money, divorce the maggot infidel, and take him for everything he was worth. Sure, the conjugal house was heavily mortgaged, but she suspected there was still at least a hundred thousand dollars of equity sitting there. Dump the trash, collect your two hundred dollars, and *DO* pass *GO*.

A wicked grin spread over her face and she rubbed her hands together, already beginning to feel better. She finished her glass of milk and stood. *Time for bed. Time for a new chapter. Time for a brand-new life.*

As she was about to go upstairs, a flash of light caught her eye from behind the sliding-glass doors leading to the backyard. Having forgotten all about the cold chill that had so rudely awakened her earlier, she turned around and approached the source of the light, hoping that it was really the guiding light. As she put both hands on the glass and peered out, a fierce wind assaulted the glass and shattered it inward with brutal force. The gale-force wind flung Giselle through the air and slammed her into the wall. As she withered down it, dazed and confused, six long glass spears impaled her, one through the heart, one through the head, and the other four pinned neatly to each extremity.

Giselle gasped and her head slumped to one side, her open mouth dribbling blood like a leaky faucet.

So swift was her demise, Giselle never even had a chance to cry for help.

Chapter Eighteen

Oliver moaned, rolled over, and eyeballed the digital alarm clock. 7:36 am. Time to get moving. He climbed out of bed with a grunt, trying to decipher the collage of erotic and violent images that had assaulted his soul in the middle of the night. He scratched his large belly, slipped into his slippers, and trudged out of the bedroom toward the bathroom. He stepped into the shower and the warm cascade of water splashing on his bulk stimulated his senses and he refocused on the images of his nightmares.

But, other than a collage of bloody murderous events intermingled with heated carnal encounters, there was nothing at all solid that he could put a finger on. No details came to mind.

Drying himself off a few minutes later, he decided to forget about the nightmares. He brushed his teeth and combed his hair, got dressed, and went into the kitchen. Sitting down at his kitchen table a few minutes later eating a bowl of Fruit Loops (he had to admit his diet hadn't changed a whole lot even though he vaguely remembered a promise he'd made to himself to clean up his act), he wondered if he should even go to work.

Carmen had dismissed him rather early yesterday. Oliver had cleaned up the glass and she'd called in a glass repair specialist. While Oliver oversaw the installation of two windows, Carmen had remained out of sight, somewhere in the kitchen doing what she later told him was "cleaning and organizing a few things."

Just before he'd left, he'd asked her if she had called her brother and sister and she'd paused, before giving him a vague response. "Don't worry, I've got everything under control."

How much control did she have? How could she have everything under control?

Becoming confused and concerned, he got up, plopped his spoon and bowl in the sink, sighed at the dirty mess, and then went into his bedroom. He studied Milton for a few seconds, still grinning amicably, yet demonically. Yet it was far too late to second-guess his new protector. Instead, Oliver gently tucked Milton away in a knapsack, carefully zipped it shut, and left for work.

Five minutes later, stuck in rush-hour gridlock on a bright sunny day, his phone rang.

It was Carmen and her voice was laced with fear. She skipped social pleasantries. "Where are you?"

"On my way to work. Stuck in gridlock traffic."

"Call in sick! I need you!"

"What... what happened?"

"My brother and sister are dead. Murdered."

"What?" Distracted and petrified, Oliver inched forward and slammed on the brakes, inches from a large truck.

The car behind him leaned on the horn, the loud and long beep drowning out Carmen's frantic words.

"Sorry," Oliver said. "I couldn't hear you."

"Never mind," Carmen said. "Call in sick and meet me at the hospital. My mother's still in Intensive Care. Room 303."

"Okay," Oliver said. "I'll be right there." But Carmen had already hung up and his last four words had been delivered to dead air space.

Oliver eventually found a break in traffic, cut down a side street, and parked. With the engine idling, he dialed work and, after a short time on hold, was patched through to supervisor Roger Richter.

"I can't come in today," Oliver said.

"Why not?"

Yesterday, the excuse he gave was the common cold, but in his panic, he forgot all about it. "My friend's brother and sister just died. She needs me."

There was a long and uncomfortable pause on the other end of the line before Roger said in an irritated tone, "Your excuses are getting better by the day, Oliver. Yesterday, it was cold, and now I guess you've miraculously healed from that and now you're saying two people have died."

"I'm serious, boss," Oliver said.

"Do you even know these people?"

"No, but..."

"How did they die?"

"I... I don't know."

"I'll tell you what, Oliver," Roger said sternly. "If you think you're sick—which we both know you're not—let me tell you something. I'm sick too. Sick of you. Don't bother returning to work. Your last check will be ready for you at Human Resources next Friday."

***

Downtrodden and disturbed, Oliver plodded down the hallway of the Toronto General Hospital almost a full hour after he'd been fired. It had taken at least thirty minutes to get to the hospital and another thirty minutes or so to find the Intensive Care Ward. He hoped Sarah's condition had improved. With everyone else dropping like flies, the last thing he wanted to see was Sarah give up the ghost. He turned a corner without looking and two orderlies whisking an elderly man in a stretcher had to veer swiftly to avoid colliding with him.

"Watch where you're going," one said, while the other shot Oliver a scowl. Even the prostrate old man started shaking his fist.

"Sorry," Oliver said, pinning himself up against the wall while the stretcher passed.

He looked both ways and felt a tap on his shoulder. He spun around, half-expecting to see Stella grinning maliciously.

But it was Carmen. Disheveled hair, bloodshot eyes, her pudgy face streaked with tears. She had black sockets under her eyes and she looked as if she'd been up all night.

"Are you okay?" Oliver said.

She grabbed him by the arm and started walking down the hall. "I've been up all night talking with cops."

"Is your mother okay?"

"I just got through with the doctor. I haven't seen her yet. He says she's still in a coma, but stabilized."

"What happened to your brother and sister?"

She stopped, squeezed his arm, and looked into his eyes pleadingly. "I'll tell you all about it later. Right now, I just want you to keep me calm. Can you do that?"

"I'll try," Oliver said.

"Look, we're not gonna stay long. My mom's in a coma anyway. After everything that's happened I just think it's more important than ever"—Carmen tapped her knapsack—"to put Grace on my mother's bedside table. Once we do that, we'll go. Okay?"

"Of course."

Two doors later, they found Room 303 and stopped. "Do you want to wait here or come in?"

"Up to you," Oliver said.

"No. It's up to you."

"I'll come in."

Carmen released Oliver's arm and he followed her into the room.

A young black-haired female nurse sat across from the bed reading Sarah's chart.

An oxygen mask covered Sarah's mouth and IVs were attached to each arm. Six small white patches with electrodes were stuck to her chest. A bank of screens stood behind and beside the bed, beeping and buzzing, monitoring Sarah's vital signs.

As Carmen and Oliver approached, the nurse stood and backed away from the chair. "You're her daughter?"

Carmen nodded.

She pointed to Oliver like he was a leper, a series of lines creasing her brow. "And who's he?"

Carmen approached the bed and cleared her throat. "He's a good friend of mine and a good friend of my mom's."

"Okay," the nurse said, not bothering to introduce herself. "I'll leave you for five minutes. That's about all I can give you." She pointed to a button attached to a cord dangling above the bed. "You see anything unusual, you press that. Okay?"

"That's fine," Carmen said. She pulled the knapsack off her back and unzipped it. She pulled out Grace. "Just so you know, this is my mom's good luck charm. She's called Grace. You don't mind if I leave her here, do you?"

The nurse headed for the door, giving Grace, Carmen, and Oliver a wide berth on her way past.

Oliver wondered if she'd been briefed on the fate of Carmen's siblings and was reacting out of fear.

The nurse stopped at the door. "That's fine. Your mother could use some luck in her condition."

Carmen brushed back a few strands of Grace's errant blonde hair and put her on the bedside table, propping her up against a lamp and pointing her smiling face toward Sarah. Then she turned around and took the bedside seat while Oliver stood at the foot of the bed and watched.

Sarah's face had shrunken since he'd last seen her. The dark circles around her eyes had widened and a few more wrinkles were visible. Yet her expression was calm and serene, her breathing steady and even.

Carmen took her mother's hand and squeezed it tenderly. "Mom, I've prayed to God that you come out of this coma. I also brought Grace in to protect you from harm. She's right at your bedside table, right here."

Oliver saw Sarah's eyelids flutter for a split-second and then close again.

Carmen saw it too and turned to Oliver. "Doctor Stevens says that although Mom's brain is functioning at a lower state of alertness, it's possible that she can understand my words. Of course, being in a coma, she wouldn't be able to respond."

"Did he say what the prognosis is?"

Carmen rolled her eyes toward her mother and Oliver took the cue. "Mom's gonna come out of this. I know she is."

Oliver nodded. He wasn't a religious man, but he decided a silent prayer was in order.

On cue, Carmen rose, pulled a second chair next to the bed, and motioned for Oliver to sit. "Let's join hands in prayer."

Oliver sat next to Carmen. She put one hand in her mother's hand, the other in Oliver's. They bowed their heads and closed their eyes and Carmen began: "Please, God, I beseech you, I beg you, please bring my mom out of this coma quickly and by your Grace grant her a speedy recovery. And please, God, protect Oliver and me from harm and destroy this evil that has recently invaded our lives. Thanks so much, oh God Almighty, and please do it quickly. Amen."

"Amen," Oliver said, raising his head and opening his eyes. As they stood up to leave, he glanced at Carmen, then at Sarah, and headed for the door. Walking down the hallway hand-in-hand with Carmen, he couldn't help wondering how swiftly his life had changed in a matter of weeks.

He was once a zombified TV and junk food addict who found vicarious carnal comfort in his dreams. Now he had to confront the grim prospect that the escapist fictional world he'd so meticulously constructed might actually be a terrifying reality. From stuffing his face with junk food, living like a self-indulgent sloth, and binge-watching B-grade horror films, now here he was, a co-star in a horror film of his own making. What a life. Carrying around magical and mysterious dolls to ward off demons and evil spirits while people in his periphery were getting murdered. He couldn't have scripted it any better if he were a horror writer. He sighed. Indeed, sometimes reality was a lot stranger than fiction.

Wait a second. Those people who died are not exactly in my periphery. They're Carmen's family members; no, they were her family members. Brother and sister. Suddenly his hand felt cold and clammy inside Carmen's and he released it with a shudder. What role did she have in all of this? Why was it that she seemed to know exactly what to do and exactly when to do it?

"What's wrong?" Carmen said as they entered the parking lot. "What're you thinking?"

Oliver offered a selective truth: "That I'm fucking terrified."

Chapter Nineteen

In the hospital parking lot, Oliver had learned that Detective Stanley Darby had driven Carmen from the interrogation room at police headquarters to the hospital. So, Oliver drove them to Carmen's house, stopping at a McDonald's and ordering two breakfast combinations. Even in times of death and crisis, people still had to eat.

They sat in Carmen's living room now, finishing off the last remnants of breakfast. All Carmen had done up to this point was bring Oliver up to speed on her mother's condition, the doctor's prognosis (that she was unlikely to snap out of the coma and it was time to start thinking about pulling the plug), and Doctor Stevens suggestion that, in any event, it was time for Carmen to invoke her POA, take control of Sarah's finances and, in the event of a miracle, start researching nursing homes. He'd made it abundantly clear that Carmen was no longer capable of giving her mother the care she needed and would need.

Oliver wanted to know about the murders and the subsequent interrogation, but he thought that he could at least wait until he'd finished his breakfast. He stuffed the last, large rectangular hash brown in his mouth, noticed Carmen watching him disapprovingly, took a small bite, and returned it to his plate. He picked up the plastic knife and fork, cut a triangular slice, and put it in his mouth. He'd have to start learning a few table manners now. He wasn't by himself in his apartment anymore, binge-watching movies and stuffing his fat face with junk food. Some things had to change if he wanted to be in the company of others.

She smiled and he returned an awkward smile.

Slicing and dicing with precise movements, Oliver finished his hash brown, being careful to chew his food slowly with his mouth closed. After he finished eating, he set down his knife and fork, picked up his large coffee, and took a sip.

Carmen had also finished her breakfast. She too took a sip from her coffee and placed it on the coffee table.

"I know what you're waiting to hear," she said, "and I'll tell you all about it."

"When did the cops call you?"

"The first call came in around midnight, I think. Maybe a little later. It was Detective Darby, telling me my brother, oh, and his girlfriend as well, had been murdered. Or it looks like murder. While I was down at the police station, I guess it was almost two in the morning by that time, Detective Darby gets another call and I learn my sister, Giselle, has also been murdered. That's when all hell broke loose, at least in my own mind. I broke down and turned into a blubbering idiot."

Many questions came to Oliver's mind, but right now the most important one seemed to be, "Do you know how they died?"

Carmen had her hands covering her face now and a few tears squeezed between her fingers. "Mark was found in the middle of the road about a hundred feet from his apartment. He'd been severely cut by glass and there were glass spears stuck all over his face and body. His girlfriend, Patricia, was found leaning out the window with multiple glass shards protruding from her face and body."

Oliver shuddered. Maybe this wasn't the time or place for this line of questioning. "We don't have to discuss this now if it's too upsetting for you."

Carmen removed a hand from her tear-stained face. "It *is* upsetting, but I want you to know so you can help me fight this. Don't you see, it looks like the demon we somehow unleashed has killed my brother, his girlfriend, and my sister? The windows, the glass, it all connects. We've already replaced two windows and we know one thing for sure—that demon likes smashing windows and using glass projectiles to kill her victims."

"Is that how your sister was killed?"

"Yeah," Carmen said, her voice laced with barely contained panic. "Her bloody sliding-glass doors imploded inward and the glass spears impaled her against a wall clear across her living room."

"Oh my God," Oliver said, feeling sweat beads pop on his forehead. He grabbed a spare McDonald's napkin and wiped them away. "Did you tell that cop anything about the dolls or the demon?"

Carmen leaned back on the armchair across from Oliver. "Are you kidding? He'd think I was crazy?"

Oliver hated to ask the next question. But he had to know. "Does Detective Darby think you're a suspect?"

"I don't think so. But he asked me a hell of a lot of questions. He may want to talk to you as well. I told him we were friends. I had to tell him the truth. And even though we have nothing to hide, we still have to get our stories straight concerning the dolls and the demons."

"You're right," Oliver said. "I won't say anything about that. Did you tell him about the windows? The ones here?"

"He knows about them. He's the same cop who showed up when my mom had a heart attack."

"Right."

"He knows that I wasn't home when Mom's bedroom window smashed, but he did ask how the upper bedroom window got broken."

"What did you say?"

"I told him I accidentally smashed it while I was vacuuming the room."

"Did he buy it?"

Carmen started pacing the room. She stopped and looked at Oliver, her youthful face creasing with worry lines. "He said something about the room looks like it's a place where satanic rituals are conducted."

"What did you say?"

"I didn't go there really. I just said my mom is into dolls and she used to like to meditate there."

"Did he buy that?"

"I doubt it, but what choice does he have? He has no evidence of satanic rituals, mysterious doll protectors, or evil bitches who go around murdering people. Even if he did, would he really want to start telling his colleagues theories like that?"

"I guess not," Oliver admitted.

Carmen continued pacing. "Look, I've got a million things to do and I'm pretty stressed out right now. I have to deal with Power of Attorney for my mother, arrange two funerals, keep Detective Darby off my back, and start looking for a nursing home for mom when, umm, *if* she recovers." She sat down beside Oliver. "I could really use your help here."

"That's why I'm here," Oliver said, pangs of sadness and compassion washing over him. "What do you want me to do?"

"Can you stay here with me for a while until things settle down? Can you call in sick for another week or two until we're sure this evil, whatever sparked it, is gone for good?"

"I can't call in sick anymore," Oliver said.

"Why not?"

"I don't have a job anymore. I got fired this morning for calling in sick."

Carmen's face brightened. "That's okay. I'll hire you. As Power of Attorney, I'm allowed to bill out for expenses. Over and above the equity in this house, Mom has a healthy bank account. You can help me find a nursing home for her. You can help me arrange the funerals. You don't need your stupid job anymore. In fact, I think I'm gonna take a leave of absence from my job until the dust settles. Under the circumstances, I don't think that would be a problem. I've got some money saved."

In spite of his earlier doubts and reservations, he put an arm around Carmen and kissed her gently on the cheek. "So, you're my new boss?"

She made a somewhat successful attempt at smiling and hugged him. "I guess I am."

Then she started pacing again. "We have to make a TO-DO list. Wait a minute. You didn't say if you'd move in here for a few days. Will you? Please, pretty please, I need you. We need each other right now, especially when you consider how much danger we're in."

Chapter Twenty

Oliver returned to Carmen's at 5:36 pm that Thursday afternoon. He'd gone home, showered and shaved, packed a few belongings, toured two nursing homes, ate at McDonald's, and now he was hiking up the walkway with a take-out bag of burgers for Carmen. He stopped at the door and twisted the old-fashioned buzzer. It made a series of muffled bell-like rings. He didn't have a key yet, and he wasn't at all comfortable enough with his new surroundings to just walk straight in.

Behind the door, he heard a deadbolt lock twist open. Carmen opened the door and waved him in.

"I need to get you a key," she said.

He kicked off his shoes and handed her the McDonald's bag. "You hungry?"

She took it. "Thanks. I'm starving. You eat?"

"Yeah."

Oliver went into the living room and slung his two knapsacks over an armchair. Carmen sat down on the couch and began munching on her Big Mac.

"Can I get a drink?" Oliver asked, wiping sweat from his brow.

Carmen pointed to the kitchen. "There's juice and Coke in the fridge and a pot of coffee if you like."

"Thanks. Can I get you anything?"

"Coke, please."

Inside the kitchen, Oliver saw papers spread out all over the kitchen table. He knew what some of them were for. Carmen had told him before he'd left that she had to make a trip to the bank with the Power of Attorney forms and get access to her mother's bank account. She'd also begun sorting through some of the details regarding funeral preparation for Giselle and Mark, and he assumed some of the paperwork must be related to that. Oliver returned to the kitchen, plopped himself down next to Carmen, and handed her a Coke, popping the cap off his at exactly the same time she did hers.

"How's your mother?" he asked, after taking a sip.

Carmen sipped her Coke and set it on the coffee table. "I have hope," Carmen said. "I talked to Doctor Stevens today and he says Mom opened her eyes again and said something. Then, I guess she drifted back into her coma, but it's a good sign."

"What did she say?"

Carmen took a bite of her Big Mac, chewed slowly, and swallowed, washing it down with more Coke. "I can't believe the doctor actually wrote it down. And it's strange."

"What is it?"

"Apparently, Mom said, 'March straight to hell, Mark and Giselle.'"

"Holy shit," Oliver said. "I guess she didn't like them much."

"It's a long story," Carmen said, putting her half-eaten burger inside its wrapper. "At one point, she thought they'd both turned out well, you know, morally upright and all that, but then when she got worse, totally immobile and everything, their visits became fewer and farther between. And their inquiries about her were far more concerned with her money than her well-being."

"That's sad," Oliver said.

"I know," Carmen said bitterly. "But now they won't get a dime. And, maybe I shouldn't have said anything, but one time I got so upset I told Mom that all they cared about was her money."

"How did that go over?"

Carmen wiped away a tear that sprouted on her lower eyelid. "Not well. Not well at all."

"And, obviously, you didn't have much of a relationship with either of them."

"No. They were jealous of my mom's affection for me. But they shouldn't have been. I'm the only one who gives a shit about her. But that's not what they thought. They thought my motivation was purely financial."

Oliver considered this for a moment, not sure what to believe at this point. Living under her roof, under her employ, and at the beginning of what he perveived was an intimate relationship, he didn't think he was in any position to begin questioning her motivation.

So instead, he asked, "Do you think your mother's somehow responsible?"

Carmen leaned back on the couch and sighed deeply. "I... I honestly don't know what to believe right now. There's still some mystery surrounding the dolls, something from my childhood that I can't remember for the life of me. It's all a big blur. But I'm confident of one thing: the dolls are good, and this force, whoever unleashed it, is pure evil."

Oliver ran a few scenarios over in his head. The one that still seemed to make the most sense was that his desperation and loneliness had unleashed it, and the dolls were certainly acting as protectors against it. Was it possible that once unleashed, Carmen's mom Sarah had somehow been able to tap into the evil force and use it to take revenge on her insensitive and uncaring children? It was totally baffling and maybe they would never know the truth. But the question remained. What to do now? He could tell by Carmen's current level of anxiety that theorizing would only make it worse. He could sense that on some level she blamed herself for this, and maybe all of her confusion stemmed from the fact that she couldn't completely clear herself.

"Why don't we take another look in that attic?" Oliver finally said. "Maybe we'll find something there that might shed some light on things."

"I really don't think I have the energy for that tonight. With everything that's been going on lately, I'm totally wiped out—mentally and physically drained."

Oliver began to realize the extent of Carmen's grief and backed off his suspicions. In a matter of days, her mother had been attacked, slipped into a coma, and was in Intensive Care. Both her brother and sister, whether she liked them or not, were now dead. And something else occurred to him, which he hadn't thought about earlier. Carmen must have had to make a trip to the morgue to identify the bodies. That would've been extremely traumatic. It was time to cut her some slack, show some compassion, and stop playing detective for at least one night.

He leaned over and touched her hand. "Why don't you go up to bed and take a nap? You've been through a lot. You've done a lot in spite of it."

Carmen yawned deeply, covering her mouth with a hand. "Ok."

He took her hand and led her upstairs. Halfway down the hall, he opened her bedroom door, led her inside, and helped her sit down on the edge of the bed. On the trip upstairs, it seemed what little color she had in her face had been replaced by a mask of white.

"Are... are you okay," he said, brushing away an errant lock of her hair.

"You're right," she said, releasing his hand. "I just need to rest. I need some time to digest all this."

Oliver went to the door. "Don't hesitate to call if you need anything."

"The worst part..." she said, a tear slipping down her cheek. "The worst part was identifying the bodies in the morgue. I didn't like them much. But I didn't hate them either, you know. They were still my brother and sister and I know on some level, I... I loved them... I love them still."

"I know," Oliver said.

"You... you forgot Isabella," Carmen said.

"Oh. I'll go get her."

***

It was already 9:30 pm and Carmen had been sleeping for about four hours. Oliver had busied himself settling into his new digs and had unpacked his knapsack in a spare upper bedroom, across the hall from the ritual room. He'd been told earlier it had been Mark's room, but he was free to use it. He sat down on the bed and unzipped the other knapsack containing Milton. He pulled the doll out slowly, brushed back his orange hair, and placed him on a dresser across from the bed, propping him up against a lamp. The Archie lookalike grinned at Oliver, making a mockery of the whole situation yet paradoxically offering protection.

Oliver examined a few glass-framed photos of Mark, mounted next to Milton. There was one of him as a boy of maybe 12, holding a bat at home plate and grinning at the camera. His grin resembled Milton's. Mocking. Another photo contained Mark, Giselle—*march straight to hell*—and Carmen kneeling down in the backyard and smiling for the camera, back-dropped by a massive rosebush below a bright blue sky. Carmen was in the center, her older brother on one side and older sister on the other. They each had a hand on her shoulder and she sat smugly, cross-legged and grinning from ear to ear.

Oliver inspected the other pictures. Racing cars. Batman and Robin. Captain America. Spiderman. The Joker, grinning maliciously.

The room was sparsely furnished. A wooden chair in the corner, a bedside table and lamp, and a large chest against a wall with a few stuffed animals on top—an elephant, a teddy bear, and Raggedy Ann. Oliver walked over to the chest and knelt down in front of it. It had been padlocked shut. His curiosity got the better of him and he pulled on the padlock. The metal latch squeaked but didn't open.

Looking around the room, he figured Carmen must've cleaned it before his arrival. It smelled of Fabreeze and the hardwood floors were dust-free and shiny. The first two dresser drawers were empty and the bottom two contained clothes, presumably Mark's. The closet door, off in a corner next to the window, was closed, the one part of the bedroom he'd yet to inspect. The window next to it was covered with Winnie-the

Pooh cloth curtains that blocked out most of the fading sunlight.

He approached the closet and opened the door. It squeaked open, revealing toys, board games, and stuffed animals, piled high. Carmen must've stuffed a lot of Mark's childhood belongings into the closet. He sat down on the single bed, looking over its length and wondering if it was too short for him. The tan bedspread smelled fresh, a floral bouquet, and the two white pillows were fluffy and new-looking. He reclined on the bed and stretched out. Sure enough, his feet hung over the edge a good six inches. He sighed. Oh well. He could always curl up in the fetal position and right now he didn't imagine it would matter much anyway. After everything that'd happened, a part of his mind was still going a million miles an hour trying to put reason to madness. Another part of his mind was adamantly telling him to give up and go with the flow. That events, as they transpired, would serve to clarify things.

He flicked on the bedside lamp, curled up in bed, and tried to calm his mind. But it wandered back to the two deaths, particularly Mark's untimely demise. Oliver couldn't help feeling guilty. He had Milton, the protective doll. He now slept in Mark's room, and he was benefiting in some serendipitous way from Sarah's money. Everything Mark probably wanted, Oliver had. He rubbed his eyes as pangs of sadness stabbed his heart. If he hadn't been such a lonely loser, none of this would've happened. He slowly descended into a black void of self-pity and reflected on the pathetic nature of his life, replaying scenes of his lonely and socially isolated existence over and over and over again in his mind; a rerun of a tragic horror movie; an unrequited love story with a pathetic protagonist; a broken record of broken dreams.

Click. Squeeeeeeeeeeeeak.

He shot out of bed, almost jumping out of his skin. He was terrified, yet in some way grateful at the abrupt interruption—a life-line out of a deep crevasse of self-pity and self-loathing. He longed for his inner turmoil to vanish like a shooting star and disappear into the black void of outer space forever and ever.

Feeling his heart begin to beat faster, he rushed to the door and opened it. He didn't remember closing it. He glanced back into the bedroom, wondering if he should bring Milton. But the bedside lamp flickered and flicked off, blanketing the bedroom in blackness. Leaving the door open a crack, in case he needed to rush back into the protective arms of Milton, he spun around, looking up and down the hallway as his heart thumped more rapidly and spasmodically. The only light he could see was a small yellow streak, poking through a crack in the door of the ritual room.

What? That was one thing he was sure about. That door had been closed the last time he'd seen it. His mind raced, an icy chill creeping up his spine. What to do? Wake up Carmen? Lock himself in Mark's room with Milton? Or enter the forbidden zone?

"Come in," a soft voice said from behind the ritual room door. "I mean you no harm."

Shivering with fear, he was about to bolt down the hall to Carmen's room, rush in, and wake her up. But something stopped him. That wasn't Stella's voice, at least not the one he remembered. *Could it be? Could it be? Selina? One of the theories, right? Selina and Stella, two sides of one spirit, trapped in purgatory, stuck in limbo in that agonizing halfway place between heaven and hell. Good and evil. Which one wins?*

He stood outside the door for a few moments, trying to steady his nerves, his breathing, his rising fear, and panic. Maybe this was his chance to be the deciding factor. Rescue the good. Destroy the evil—Oliver the hero.

On shaky legs, he stepped forward, and with an unsteady hand, he pushed the door open. It creaked, long and whiney, before bumping into the bedroom wall. He studied the table in the center of the room. The two chairs. The candle. The steel box. The doll-decorated mirrored vanity. Everything looked as it should be.

But wait. Above the table, he saw a yellow glow rise and envelop the upper half of the room.

Against his better judgment, he stepped inside.

The yellow glow shifted and the room turned a foggy gray, walled with large boulders, dungeon-like. Then the fog lifted and he saw her clearly, chained against the wall, naked, blood dripping from her breasts. Tall. Shapely. Long black hair, dark eyes, smooth, olive-toned complexion with petite facial features, and perfect white teeth.

Selina looked at Oliver with sad eyes. "Help me. You're the only one who can help me."

Oliver took two steps forward and stopped ten feet from the captive and tortured woman. "You're Selina, the woman of my dreams."

"I am," she said, trying but failing to smile.

"From whom do I need to save you?" Oliver asked.

"From Stella."

"I thought you were Stella."

A blood-red tear snaked down Selina's cheek. "I am. Save me from myself. Pleeeeeeeeease!"

His arms outstretched, Oliver rushed toward her and tried to wrap her in an embrace. But the entire scene including Selina vanished in a flash and Oliver ended up hugging himself, spinning around, tripping over his toes, and falling on his ass on the hardwood floor.

"Oww... Shit, fuck, shit," Oliver said.

"What's wrong?"

Oliver saw Carmen standing in the doorway, a look of bewilderment on her face. She rushed into the room and helped him to his feet. "What happened?"

"I saw her."

"Saw who?"

"Selina. It's true what we thought. Selina and Stella are one and the same. Good and evil."

"Tell me this downstairs over hot chocolate," Carmen said.

Closing the door securely behind her, she led Oliver downstairs.

Over hot chocolates a few minutes later, he explained the whole story to her, providing a full description of Selina, but omitting his descent into guilt, shame, self-loathing, and self-pity.

Sitting across from him, Carmen tucked an errant lock of hair behind her ear and took a sip of hot chocolate. "I've got news for you, and I'm not sure you're gonna like it."

Oliver couldn't help but notice that Carmen had changed into a flowery pink nightgown with a plunging neckline that left little to the imagination, at least as far as her bosom was concerned. Every time she leaned over to sip her hot drink, one of her large breasts strained to escape the night gown's neckline. She seemed unfazed by it.

"What's that?" Oliver said.

"I had a dream during that nap. I dreamt I was Selina and I had escaped my chains and was kicking the shit out of Stella."

"Wow. Weird. How did it end?"

"I dunno. I heard voices coming from the ritual room and woke up."

"Holy shit, that *is* strange," Oliver said. "Especially when you consider that while you were dreaming you were Selina I *saw* Selina. And, in my, err vision, I don't know what to call it, Selina had momentarily escaped Stella's clutches and was actively trying to recruit my help to purge her from evil. What do you make of it?"

"I don't know. But I know Freud would have a field-day with it."

"It tells us that we're on the right track with this Selina-Stella theory of good and evil. Both two extremes of the same person, same spirit, whatever she is."

"There's something else," Carmen said, lifting her mug and again exposing a generous amount of cleavage. "It all makes some kind of weird sense. If, as we thought, and my mother thought, Stella was possessing me, it would stand to reason that if Stella and Selina are both the same entity, then I'd also have to eventually see Selina. I guess she's the weaker force right now and that explains why I see her in my dreams and we, mostly you, see Stella in the waking world."

"Now I see both of them in the waking world," Oliver said. "But I see your point, and it does make sense."

"Interesting. I wonder how we can ultimately purge Selina of her evil side."

"How about the obvious?" Oliver said. "Another ritual in the ritual room. I mean that's where Selina showed up. That room can expel evil, like it did to Stella, and attract good."

Carmen's brow wrinkled and she scanned the ceiling as if it were an entryway for spirits or demons. "Okay, when do you want to do that?"

"Well, no time..."

Carmen's cellphone rang and they both started.

As Carmen answered the phone, Oliver watched goosebumps crawling up her bare arms and legs. Her nipples hardened and poked the sheer cotton fabric of the nightgown. Her breasts also heaved outward, straining the fabric and practically begging to be unleashed into the world, at least into Oliver's waiting and wanting mouth.

He felt a tingling in his crotch and he remembered that very recent, very pleasurable hand-job—Carmen's so-called defense tactic against the evil Stella. Would she employ it again tonight? Doubtful. That was before he had Milton for protection. Shit. With his new guardian angel, she wouldn't have any reason to gratify him. Unless she was as horny as he was right now.

He stepped out of his sexual fantasy, and back into reality, picking up the tail end of Carmen's conversation.

"That's great news, Doctor Stevens. Yes, I know it's too late tonight, but I'll be in first thing tomorrow to see her. Thank you so, so much."

Carmen lunged off the couch and dove on Oliver, landing in his lap and wrapping him in a tight embrace. He felt her nipples stiffen even more as they poked into his chest.

"You'll never believe it," Carmen said, kissing him on the cheek. "Mom came out of her coma! She's talking. She's making sense."

"Wow, that's great!" Oliver said, taking advantage of the unforeseen opportunity to wrap Carmen in a tight embrace.

After a moment, she stared at him self-consciously and climbed off his lap. "My God, you must think I'm some kind of evil seductress. Look at me, showing my boobs and crawling all over you."

"I was kind of enjoying it."

"I'm sure you were." Carmen strutted toward the kitchen and stopped at the door. "This calls for a nightcap before bed. What'll it be? A shot of Scotch, or a glass of wine?"

Wine is panty-remover. Is she even wearing any panties? I didn't feel any. "I'll have the wine, please."

"Good choice."

She emerged from the kitchen with two full glasses of white wine, handed one to Oliver, and sat down across from him on an armchair, tugging up her nightgown as soon as the cleavage started to show. She also made a point of curling up her legs on the couch and closing them tightly.

"Wanna come with me tomorrow to visit Mom?"

"Sure."

She leaned toward Oliver and raised her glass. "To Mom's full recovery. Thank you. Thank you, God, for answering my prayers."

They clinked glasses and Oliver said, "And to our recovery."

"Amen," she said.

***

After about an hour of light-hearted conversation, albeit absent of a few laughs, they decided to turn in for the night. The events had taken a toll on them and Carmen still professed to being quite exhausted, also claiming the glass of wine had gone to her head. And although Oliver felt he wouldn't be able to sleep because of everything that had happened, he knew he needed to try if he wanted to be in top form for the visit with Sarah tomorrow.

Oliver trailing, they walked down the hall. Carmen stopped at the first door and turned around to face him. "Have you been in this room?"

"No."

"This was Giselle's room. Still has all her stuff in it. I haven't cleaned it out yet. Maybe tomorrow."

"Maybe tomorrow," Oliver agreed. "But you cleaned out Mark's room a bit."

"Yeah."

They continued on and she stopped in front of her bedroom door. She gave him a look, equal parts expectant and worried. "I don't know what to do. If we have any attraction, I don't want it to be instigated by what's been happening. You know, Selina and Stella. Yet, after what happened, I don't know how comfortable you'd be in Mark's room. And I'm also afraid that even though you have Milton for protection, Stella might come and try and attack you."

"It's up to you," Oliver said. "I can get Milton and sleep on the sofa downstairs. That bed in Mark's room is a little small for me anyway."

"I should've thought of that," Carmen said, opening her bedroom door.

Oliver peered in, noticing a subtle yellow glow from the nightstand lamp illuminating Isabella. She was propped up on the nightstand facing the door, grinning and wordlessly inviting them in.

"Okay," Carmen said. "You take the couch, and I'll see you in the morning. Have a good night."

Oliver stood there for an awkward moment staring at Carmen before finally turning and walking away. He stopped and looked back. Carmen was halfway in her bedroom, her head and shoulder leaning out from the doorway.

"Have a good night," Oliver said.

She closed the door with a meaningful *click*.

Inside Mark's room, Oliver quickly grabbed Milton, headed for the door, and closed it tightly behind him. He checked the ritual room and sighed when he realized that, yes, the door was still closed. Just the way they'd left it. He felt a surface temptation to fling the door open to see if Selina still required his knight-in-shining-armor services. He'd like to rescue that delicious soul in more ways than one. But he pushed the fleeting notion aside and headed down the hall, lit by a glowing red nightlight plugged into a wall outlet right outside Carmen's door.

As Oliver went past it, he heard a soft voice, "Come in."

He stopped, studied the closed door, and listened. Nothing. Silence.

He stood there for a full minute listening for another invite. But none came and he put one foot in front of the other, ready to head downstairs, even though he was as horny as a polecat.

The door creaked open and Oliver froze. His body tingled all over from the anticipation. He felt no fear at all, only an eerie déjà vu that it was finally time to realize his lifelong dream for love, acceptance, and the beautiful calming bliss and subsequent serenity that only carnality and lust could usher in.

Oliver stepped inside the room. A halo of misty yellow light surrounded the bed and he couldn't see Carmen. He forced his feet forward, set Milton on a nearby dresser, and spun around, filled with excitement and longing.

The yellow fog above the bed began to lift, revealing Carmen, *no Selina*, lying spread-eagle, naked and ready. Her black eyes sparkled as the view became clearer.

Oliver moved closer to the bed, stopping at the foot of it, eagerly anticipating what was to come next. His mouth fell open and a drop of saliva dribbled down his chin—a rabid wolf frothing at the mouth.

His tent-pole stood at full mast, straining to escape from his cotton sweatpants. He watched Selina's hand glide over her death-defying breasts, tweak both nipples erect, and then move down to her dripping wet mound. She slowly and seductively inserted a finger and moaned with pleasure, long and loud.

Oliver wasted no time. He stripped off his sweatpants, frantically removed his socks, practically tore off his T-shirt, and climbed into bed. He glided his tongue along Selina's shapely leg, moving slowing up to her shaven pussy. When he reached it, she removed her moist finger and he inserted his tongue into her vagina. She moaned softly as he probed her love-juice-lathered love canal.

Before long, she grabbed his hair with both hands, pressed his face into her vagina, stiffened and bucked, and then began shaking uncontrollably.

Only when he heard a long and satisfying moan did he come up for air, lick his lips, and admire Selina's beautiful face. Her eyes were closed. She was lost in an otherworldly bliss.

Then she opened her eyes and scrutinized him soberly. This time it was Carmen's voice. "What're you doing?"

"Uh... I think I've already done it."

"Oh my God," Carmen said, wrapping him in a tight embrace. "I thought it was a dream."

"Me too at first," Oliver said. "But it's a dream come true."

Chapter Twenty-One

Before heading to the hospital that balmy Friday afternoon, Carmen and Oliver had discussed the unplanned but mutually pleasurable events of last night. An hour of discussion had produced a consensus—no point fighting what they couldn't control. If they needed to have sex to keep evil spirits away, so be it. If they needed to make love to separate the benevolent Selina from Stella, her evil alter-ego, then go with the flow. They'd decided the rest—relation-forming chemistry, mutual attraction, love, and respect—would either happen naturally or it wouldn't. They knew one thing for sure, it wouldn't be for lack of trying, while at the same time trying to contain and destroy their demons.

Walking down a hallway of the hospital with Carmen, Oliver felt uneasy, a sense of foreboding that what waited for them behind the door to Sarah's new room was a different kettle of fish. Her knowledge and use of the dolls, her psychic ability, and the irony that while her daughter, son, and his girlfriend had been brutally murdered by an unknown and probably supernatural perpetrator, Sarah had been given a new lease on life. What did she know about their deaths? Did Sarah, in her comatose state, enter that mysterious crossroads between the living and the dead and murder three people? *Don't be silly, it was Stella.* But Oliver had run out of time for an in-depth analysis, not that it had gotten him anywhere in the past anyway.

They arrived at the door to Sarah's new room. 606.

Carmen touched his hand gently. "What's wrong? You look like you've seen a ghost?"

"I... I don't like hospitals."

"Who does? Listen, my mom is in a fragile state, so don't say anything about the deaths right now. Okay?"

"I'll leave that up to you," Oliver said, feeling his palms grow sweaty.

"I'm not gonna mention it, but I will gently suggest a nursing home."

Oliver nodded. The two he'd viewed Thursday had seemed okay, but an incident with a patient care aide at one, verbally abusing a resident, and a caustic attitude by the administrator at the other—"You should've booked an appointment first"—suggested they needed to keep looking. Earlier in the day while doing an internet search, they'd discovered King's Garden long-term care facility in Hamilton, Ontario, 45 minutes away, and Carmen had thought it would be the perfect fit. Great online reviews and far enough away from all the trouble in Toronto. Oliver hadn't mentioned the long commute concerning visits. He suspected Carmen also had a plan for that but had yet to make him privy to it.

"You ready?" Carmen said, searching his eyes.

Oliver noticed a twinkle in those eyes that had been absent in the past. "Sure."

Carmen pushed the door. On smooth-sailing hydraulic hinges, it slowly glided open and stopped an inch or so from the wall-mounted doorstop.

The first thing Oliver saw was Grace, propped on a nightstand beside Sarah's bed. He imagined her interrogative eyes giving him the once over.

Then he saw Sarah, propped up in bed, looking hopefully at them. For just a fraction of a second, Oliver saw Sarah transform into Stella, grinning maniacally and beckoning him forward with an outstretched, curling index finger. He blinked several times, opened his eyes, and Stella disappeared, replaced by Sarah.

They entered the room and Oliver sat down nervously on one of the two chairs positioned bedside, as if Sarah had been expecting them.

"Mom, you look great," Carmen said.

"So do you, my dear," Sarah said, arching an eyebrow knowingly. "You're positively glowing today."

Carmen immediately leaned over and kissed her mother on the cheek, giving her a warm hug and rubbing her arm tenderly before taking a seat.

Carmen hadn't been exaggerating, Oliver realized. Sarah's face looked ten years younger and she looked like she'd shed a dozen wrinkles. The dark circles under her eyes had shrunk noticeably and her eyes possessed a sparkle and vitality that hadn't been there before.

Oliver acknowledged Sarah with, "Hello, Ms. Weathersby, great to see you've recovered so quickly."

She offered him a nod and a cheerful smile.

"How do you feel, Mom?" Carmen said.

"Don't care much for the food in here," she said, pointing to a plate of partially eaten meatloaf on a bedside tray. "But otherwise, glad to be alive. That was a close one."

"You look terrific, Mom. I... I just can't get over it."

"How's everything at the house?"

"Fine."

"I... I miss it."

"I imagine you would. But with things the way they are, and your precarious situation, I really think it's time we started looking at some long-term care for you."

Sarah scratched her head slowly and frowned. "We never want to face that point in our lives, do we? The point where we become a burden to our children and can't look after ourselves anymore. I guess at some point we all have to."

"We do," Sarah agreed.

"We'll all be there one day," Oliver said.

Sarah continued: "I've been thinking for some time now that I was becoming a burden to you. And now that you've found a man, and a nice man at that, I guess you'll need more freedom to start living your own life and pursuing your own dreams, instead of watching over and caring for me around the clock..."

Sarah trailed off and looked out a sunlit window as a crow swooped past and then soared up into the heavens.

"Mom... we're not exactly an item."

"Oh, don't kid yourself, my dear. A mother knows these things. I assume you've taken control of Power of Attorney after I slipped into a coma."

Carmen nodded and blushed.

"Good. It'll make it a lot easier for you to pay the bills. How're Giselle and M..." The color rushed from Sarah's face. She tilted her head forward, covering her face with both hands.

Oliver thought he saw a tear squirt between her fingers and snake its way down the back of her hand but he couldn't be sure. He couldn't be sure of anything right now.

Sarah opened two fingers, exposing one gray eye. "Tell me it was just a dream."

"What're you talking about, Mom?"

Sarah dropped her arms resignedly. "When I was in a coma, I had a dream, or a vision, that they were murdered." She sighed deeply and continued. "I saw Mark and his girlfriend get killed first. Then Giselle, pinned horribly to her wall by large glass spears."

Oliver shuddered. *My God, she knows. Did she do it?*

Even Carmen's blush was chased away by a white storm at her mother's revelation.

"And I... and I was powerless to do anything about it," Sarah said.

Carmen leaned over and gently stroked her mother's shoulder. "It wasn't you, Mom. It was that evil Stella."

"I know," Sarah said matter-of-factly. "I was the one who told you about her. Remember?"

"I do, Mother. And if it wasn't for you we probably wouldn't be here right now. Do you know when you'll be released?"

"The doctor says, if I continue to improve, maybe in another week. I feel so sad about Mark and Giselle, really. I mean, I know once I got older they cared less and less about me."

"They cared about your money, Mom."

"Well, that doesn't change the fact they were my children. A mother hates to lose her children before she goes."

"I know, Mom. I'm upset over it as well. We have to get on the best we can now. I'll have to see to the details of their funerals in the coming days, but I can't even think about it now.

Death certificates and all that. Clearing out possessions from their homes. It all seems overwhelming. And my first priority is to get you into a nursing home."

"Have you seen any?" Sarah asked.

"Two. Oliver did. He's helping me. He didn't like them so we're moving on. We have another one to look at in Hamilton this evening."

"What's it called?"

"King's Garden."

"I've heard of it," Sarah said. "Supposed to be a pretty good place."

"Anyway, we'll check it out and let you know." Carmen stood. "We should go now, Mom. Lots to do." Carmen adjusted Grace, pointing her face toward her mother. "You've got her to protect you."

"I do," Sarah said. "She already saved me once. When... Stella came after me."

Carmen reached over her shoulder and grabbed her knapsack, pulling it partway off her back, unzipping it, and pulling Isabella's head out. "We don't leave home without them. Oliver's got Milton."

Sarah looked from Carmen to Oliver.

Oliver managed a weak smile and tapped his knapsack. "Safe and sound. Right here."

"He'll keep you safe and sound," Sarah said.

"That's a fact," Oliver said, standing up.

Carmen leaned over and kissed her mother on the cheek. "We'll see you tomorrow, Mom. Do you need anything?"

"Pack a few clothes for me when I get outta here. And some slippers."

"Okay."

"I just have one question, Sarah?" Oliver said. "When you were in a coma, did you see a white light?" As soon as he said it, he realized how stupid it was. She'd just said she witnessed three brutal murders. If that represented a white light then the symbolic colors for good and evil had mysteriously changed.

"No," Sarah said. "All black, terrifying, and confusing."

***

Approaching the sliding-glass doors to the hospital exit, Carmen felt a tap on her shoulder. She spun around and recognized Doctor Stevens instantly.

"Where are you going?" Doctor Stevens said, studying them through black-framed spectacles with magnifying glasses for lenses.

"We're going to check out a nursing home for my mother," Carmen said.

The doctor looked puzzled for a second but then gave them a knowing look. "Of course you are. But I wanna see you later in my office. Both of you."

"What?" Oliver said, while Carmen gave the doctor a bewildered look.

But he spun around and scurried away before they could say more.

"What's with him?" Oliver asked when they reached the parking lot.

"Who knows? But I'm not gonna worry about it. We've got enough shit on our plates right now to worry about him."

Chapter Twenty-Two

Oliver didn't understand why Carmen had postponed the appointment with King's Garden nursing home, rescheduling it for the following Monday. Driving her black Toyota Camry, she had been about to merge onto the busy 401 freeway to Hamilton but suddenly pulled over, called the nursing home, and canceled the appointment.

When he'd asked about it, she'd glared at him and said, "I'm not in the fucking mood right now. How about that?"

Now, here they were, driving around Toronto, presumably heading to Carmen's house, and she'd grown quiet and detached. Sensing the sudden mood shift, Oliver had kept his mouth shut, too afraid to say anything for fear of a tongue lashing.

It was pitch-black outside by the time they'd arrived at Carmen's house. She parked the car curbside, got out, and slammed the door abruptly, forgetting all about her knapsack containing Isabella, her protector.

She marched up to the house and spun around on the porch.

"Are you coming, or are you gonna sit there all day?" she said.

Oliver opened his mouth to respond but noticed she'd already disappeared inside the house, slamming the door behind her.

He looked at the house and then had to do a double-take. The bright orange brick suddenly turned black, and the pitched roof elongated garishly. A light in an upper bedroom went on, then another, and then the porchlight illuminated, giving the appearance of two white eyes and a white nose. All that was missing was the mouth. But as Oliver stared at the house, mesmerized and terrified, the porch sprouted razor-sharp, blood-stained fangs. Then a mouth grew and stretched. Soon it was hovering over the Camry, drenching the car in a fountain of blood.

"What the fuck," Oliver said, grabbing Carmen's knapsack and exploding out of the vehicle. His feet hit the curb running and he raced down the block. At about the halfway point, he glanced back, expecting to see the house-turned-monster hovering above him, those blood-stained fangs about to devour him for lunch. But the house looked normal. No bedroom lights on. No gaping mouth with deadly fangs. Only the small porchlight gleamed invitingly.

He stopped quickly, caught his breath, and continued to watch the house for signs of a terrifying transformation.

"Get your shit together," he said after a few moments.

And although it took five more minutes of self-convincing before he could return to the porch, he still recognized that something was wrong. The house transformation may have been his imagination, which he doubted, but there was definitely something wrong with Carmen. He took a deep breath, turned the front door handle, and pulled. Nothing happened. The door was locked.

He banged on it. "Carmen, open up. You locked me out."

He heard the deadbolt twisting. The door opened and Carmen looked at him curiously. "What're you doing outside?"

She looked very much herself now. *Good.* "You... you locked me out."

"What the hell was I thinking?" she said, giving herself a mock slap upside the head. "Come on in. You live here now. This is your house."

"You forgot something," Oliver said, offering her the knapsack.

"Jesus H. Christ," she said, taking it. "What's wrong with me? How could I forget Isabella?"

Carmen went into the living room, tossed the knapsack on an armchair, and sat down on the couch.

As Oliver entered the room, he noticed a bottle of Scotch on the table, two glasses beside it, and one half-full. Carmen picked up her glass and drained it in one long gulp. Then she burped loudly. "Sorry, but I needed that."

She patted the spot beside her seductively. "Well, don't be shy. Come and join me for a drink." She gazed at the ceiling, her eyes moving rapidly as if she was realizing something was wrong but yet powerless to control it. Then her contours returned to normal.

"Don't just stand there," she said. "Get your fat ass over here."

He complied, too afraid to do anything else. And, if he had to be completely honest with himself, there was a morbid fascination with this new-and-not-so-improved version of Carmen. Confident, cocky, in your face, and he had an idea where it was leading.

He sat down next to her and she refilled her glass. Then she topped up his untouched glass.

"No point toasting to anything," she said, raising the glass. "Let's just drink for the sake of drinking and drink to get drunk." She tipped the glass to her lips, which had grown full and red, and gulped. She stopped when she noticed Oliver not drinking.

Only staring wide-eyed and horrified.

Setting her glass down, she said, "Now, be a good boy and join me."

As he reached for his glass, she got to it first, brought it up to his lips, cranked open his jaw with the other hand, and poured. Half of the potent golden liquid slid down his throat, the other half dribbled down his chin, neck, and shirt.

He began coughing and she stood. "Oh, you'll be okay. Don't be a baby, now."

He'd set the knapsack containing Milton next to him and she leaned over and swiftly grabbed it.

"What're you doing?" he said.

But she'd already picked up the other rucksack containing Isabella and was rushing up the stairs. She stopped. "We don't need them right now. I'm putting them away. Stay put. I've got a surprise for you."

Oliver heard her shuffling around upstairs and thought of fleeing the house that instant. But he couldn't bring himself to lift a foot or a finger. He was too far gone for that now.

Five minutes later, his eyes popped open and his penis snapped to attention when he saw Stella slowly shuffling down the stairs. She wore a black bodysuit and carried a long black whip, curling it around her arm as she descended.

She reached the bottom and grinned evilly at him. "I've got control now and you'll damn well do what I say."

Stella glided smoothly over to the couch and stopped a few feet in front of Oliver. "Take off your shirt," she demanded.

He complied.

"Now stand up."

He did.

"Take off your pants."

He stripped down to his gray boxers.

"Now your socks."

He peeled them off. "You're not gonna hurt me, are you?"

She stepped back and snapped the whip. The tip of it struck his stomach and tore a three-inch gash immediately. Blood sprayed out.

"Oww," Oliver said. "Don't hurt me." He was rapidly becoming frightened; the morbid fascination washed away by the sharp pain and blood droplets spraying the carpet, staining his stomach and boxers red.

Oliver saw red. Red rage. "Fuck you," he said, pushing Stella hard with both hands. "I don't want you. I want Selina, err, Carmen. The real Carmen."

Stella staggered back but quickly regained her balance. "Selina's long gone. Carmen's long gone. I'm the new kid on the block. I'm the girl next door."

Oliver seized the small opening that he had and ran for the stairs. He heard the crack of the whip and felt a stinging pain on his ankle as he scrambled up, but he didn't stop. He hit the upper-floor hallway running, raced down to the end of the hall, jerked open the ritual room door, and slammed it shut, pinning his body against it and panting for breath while he searched for the dolls.

He heard pounding on the door as he scanned the room. With every beat, the door opened an inch or so and he had to continue to press the full bulk of his weight against it each time to prevent it from flying open.

He spotted the dolls, right where they should be, he supposed. But Stella had positioned them incestuously, with Isabella mounted atop a grinning Milton while she pounded furiously away at him. *Keep it in the family,* Oliver thought, and had to stifle a maniacal laugh.

Stella pounded on the door some more and he continued to press up against it. But he was losing the battle. It was only a matter of time before it sprang open with brutal force and sent him soaring across the room.

He had one plan and one chance to execute it. Run for the dolls and, when the door burst open, thrust them in Stella's face. They'd worked before. They should again. He waited for a pause in the thumping, a split second between thuds, and he leaped for the dolls.

As the door sprang open, the bottom hinges giving way, Stella burst into the room.

Oliver grabbed Isabella and Milton by their necks, spun around, and backed into the wall as Stella charged.

As she closed the gap quickly, he thrust both dolls in her face. Isabella struck her on one side of the face, Milton on the other.

The blows stopped her in her tracks and she hissed loudly, before grimacing in pain and wilting to the floor.

Oliver watched as Stella slowly transformed. The whip disappeared, along with the bodysuit, and now it was only Carmen, completely naked, hugging herself tightly in a fetal position and balling her eyes out.

Oliver dropped to his knees, setting the dolls next to him. He leaned over and gently stroked Carmen's sweat-soaked hair.

"It's okay, honey. She's gone now. Everything's gonna be okay. I promise."

***

Everything was okay, or at least felt okay, after Stella's unpredictable and violent attack. Oliver had helped Carmen up, draped her nakedness in one of his oversized T-shirts, and escorted her to bed. After retrieving Isabella and positioning her on Carmen's bedside table, he'd tucked her in, given the traumatized woman a friendly but cautious kiss on the cheek, and left the room, deciding that, at least for tonight, the sofa was far safer than her bed.

He'd brought down Milton, positioned him near the couch, and went about disinfecting and bandaging his surprisingly superficial stomach and ankle wounds. He also wiped most of the blood droplets off the floor and little throw rug underneath the living room coffee table.

As he curled up on the sofa a few hours later, he started to realize that his level of fear had begun to decline. In theory, he should be in shock and still be terrified after such an attack. But it had become the new normal and, like it or not, he had to steel himself to be able to fight his way through it. With any luck, they'd turn a corner soon and put this evil behind them once and for all. He drifted off with the knowledge that they still had a few aces up their sleeves. They had the dolls, they had the ritual room, and they had their determination to survive and thrive.

Chapter Twenty-Three

Tuesday afternoon. Three days of relative calm and harmony had passed. Oliver was busy in the living room removing framed pictures from the wall, many of them shots of Carmen and her family. Some were group photos with the three children and her mother. A few shots of all three children playing amicably in the garden together. Absent was Matheson, her father. Oliver surmised that was probably by design. Sarah had likely been extremely traumatized by the untimely passing of her husband and had perhaps wisely decided against such daily reminders. A number of pictures of Mark alone and Giselle alone. A few pictures of Sarah in her much younger days, an attractive and confident woman. But Carmen had insisted they all be boxed and stored. The living room, according to her, looked like a grandmother's house and, "We live here now and need a younger and fresher look."

Carmen tended to work in the kitchen and she had assigned Oliver the living room. He occasionally overheard her on the phone, arranging for Giselle and Mark's funeral, delegating details of clearing out their worldly possessions, sorting out their wills (both up to their eyeballs in debt), and sometimes talking to her mother on the phone. According to Doctor Stevens, Sarah would be released on Friday so they had rescheduled a tour of King's Garden nursing home for Wednesday, tomorrow. Carmen had changed the appointment three times and although he was mystified at her reluctance to visit the facility, he'd managed to put it out of his mind since he could see definite signs that his relationship with Carmen was starting to flourish naturally and organically. Oliver didn't want to throw a monkey wrench in the middle of that harmony.

He put the last picture in the box—"I want all of them gone," Carmen had said—taped it shut and moved on to an antique sofa in a corner of a room that nobody ever seemed to sit on. The reason, according to Carmen, was that it was covered in its original factory plastic and her mother had insisted the protective layer stay on.

Well not anymore. Oliver found his exacto knife and began carefully slicing and peeling away the plastic layer. When he got it all off, he put it in a garbage bag and stood back to admire the piece. It was either a replica or an original chaise lounge chair, a psychiatrist's sofa, upholstered in black, button-down leather. *A magnificent piece really*, Oliver thought, also realizing at the same time why nobody wanted to use it—too afraid of being psychoanalyzed and perhaps labeled. He pulled the sofa away from the wall to the place where Carmen had instructed him to put it, in between the armchair and sofa so that it would close the living room seating area in and offer a sense of community and friendliness. That is, of course, if you could look past the function and purpose of such a sofa.

Oliver sat down on it. *On the other hand, it's not a bad thing to admit your personality disorders and recruit the services of a shrink to help you overcome them. Actually, it takes a lot of courage.* He sighed, stretched out, closed his eyes, and enjoyed the moment, feeling the afternoon sunshine beaming through the open living room bay window and warming his soul. He heard the mumblings of a conversation echoing from the kitchen, but the volume was too low to decipher the words.

And it didn't matter. He was growing more and more confident by the day in Carmen's competency to take care of business.

"Do you want my diagnosis?"

He opened his eyes and saw Carmen standing in the living room. She still wore his oversized white T-shirt and also had on a pair of baggy yellow sweat pants, the knees dirt-stained from scrubbing the kitchen floor earlier that day. Her hair was neatly tied back in a ponytail, held together by a matching yellow ribbon. Coordinating the color-coded ensemble, she held a yellow feather-tipped duster in one hand. Her face was vibrant with color and vitality, her deep brown eyes clear, focused, and lucid.

"Sure," Oliver said

She set down the duster and sat in the armchair. Then she crossed her legs and feigned writing something on an imaginary pad with an imaginary pen. After a moment, she put down the make-believe items, scrunched her face, and scratched her chin. "You're an anti-social, socially awkward recluse with a propensity for selfishness and self-gratification. You're also, at least you were, addicted to junk food and binge-watching horror movies. And you have, or at least had, low self-esteem."

"Wow," Oliver said. *At least she didn't say loser.* "Is that all?"

Carmen picked up her note pad, or maybe it was a file a mile long. "In the past, you used to repress your feelings and were incapable of having an intimate relationship. Too many broken hearts, I suspect. You also have obsessive-compulsive tendencies and had all but given up on society at large until I came along."

Oliver sat up, stunned by Carmen's accuracy. "I'd be lying if I said you didn't hit the nail on the head. Tell me, doctor, does that make me a complete lunatic?"

"No. It just means that you have a number of issues to work through and, with my help, you are working through them. Wanna do me?"

He did. But not necessarily the way she meant. He hadn't touched her intimately in three days, and the earlier passionate sexual encounters had awakened long-dormant sexual needs. *You forgot sexually repressed. Even fat slob. Is that even a psychiatric diagnosis? What about my personal hygiene issues? Never mind. That was then, this is now.*

He rose from the couch. "Sure, I'll do you. But we have to change places."

"Okay."

They switched places and Oliver copied Carmen's earlier pose. After a moment of thought, he scratched his chin, deciding in favor of downplaying what he viewed as Carmen's personality disorders. Discretion was always better. And besides, he was no expert. He had enough problems of his own, as she had so accurately observed. He didn't want to detonate this new equilibrium and chemistry that had begun to grow.

Possessed, obsessed, paranoid schizophrenic with a propensity for violence. "You're a loner and a recluse who'd practically given up on humanity until I came along. You're also strong-willed, independent, and intelligent."

Carmen sat up and waved a finger. "Wait a second. You're sugar-coating it. And those last three things aren't personality disorders or mental illnesses. They're attributes."

"They're true though," Oliver said. And he believed they were. Besides, the possessed-obsessed- paranoid-schizophrenic-with-a-propensity-for-violence might be all Stella's doing. It probably wasn't who Carmen really was. Satisfied with his rationale, he decided to leave it alone.

"Is that all there is?"

"For this session, yes," Oliver said. "If you wanna know more, you'll have to make an appointment for next week. Same time, same place."

Carmen laughed. "Okay, doctor, and guess what?"

"What?"

"You're pretty accurate there."

"Thanks."

"My pleasure, doctor."

Oliver hoped the 'doctor' title wouldn't stick. Along with his hatred of hospitals, he harbored a strong dislike for doctors.

Carmen got up and walked toward the kitchen, stopping, and turning around. "I have some work to finish up. What do you wanna do for dinner later? I've been so busy I hadn't planned anything."

"How about we go out for dinner?" Oliver said. "On me. You like Chinese?"

"Love it. Sounds great." Carmen was about to turn around, but then she stopped. "I almost forgot. I've got some good news for you."

"Oh?" Oliver said, raising an eyebrow.

"I just got off the phone with Detective Darby. We're completely in the clear and he won't even bother talking to you."

"Good."

"He tells me the files are still open but he's not actively investigating them. You know what I think?"

"What?"

"He's realized, because of the nature of the murders, he can't possibly pin them on a human. And to pursue the supernatural would make him the laughing stock of his colleagues. He's fucked, either way you slice it."

***

Even though they'd enjoyed a delicious Chinese food dinner, even though that day and evening—aside from the clinical diagnoses—had gone as smooth as silk, they'd mutually decided that it was time to act. The calm surely wouldn't last forever. Not with Stella looming in the shadowy backdrop, ready to pounce at the first opportunity. It was tenuous tranquility, they knew, the proverbial and cliché calm before the storm.

Surrounded by candlelight, the ritual room window ajar to release the evil spirits, they sat around the table holding hands. Beside Carmen, Isabella sat ready and waiting behind a small glowing candle. Beside Oliver, Milton stood behind a small candle, prepared for an exorcism of sorts. In the middle of the table sat the sacred and mysterious closed book, on top of which stood another candle. Carmen no longer needed to read from the book. Returning from dinner, she'd read and memorized the applicable passages and knew them by heart. Nothing would be left to chance. She knew exactly what to do.

It was exactly midnight and the light of the full moon shone brilliantly through the open window, casting a surreal and ceremonial glow.

They planned on saying silent prayers before the audible invocations and prayers would commence.

Oliver released Carmen's hands and positioned his for prayer. He watched Carmen do the same thing. In a matter of days, he'd converted to his own version of Christianity, encouraged and applauded by Carmen, who'd said his conversion would give them more things in common, more possibilities that their newly formed union might be successful. Also, his new-found faith would add a new weapon to their evil-destroying arsenal.

"Are you ready?" she asked.

"Yes," he said.

"Let's begin."

They simultaneously closed their eyes.

Oliver prayed silently: *Please, God, rid the world of this evil pestilence. Banish evil Stella to the bowels of hell forever, give peace and harmony to Carmen and me and Sarah. Please, God, let our love grow stronger and bless us with good health and everlasting peace, harmony, and happiness. But first, please, God, oh, I beg you, get rid of Stella and rid us of this evil curse. Thank you, Lord.*

"Amen," Oliver said, opening his eyes.

"Amen," Carmen said, opening her eyes.

They rejoined their hands.

"I'm gonna say the evil-cleansing chant right now," Carmen said. "We keep our eyes open for some of it. At some point, and I'll wink when it's time, we have to close our eyes. Okay?"

"Got it."

They locked eyes and Carmen commenced: "Oh, God Almighty, please hear my prayers. Please answer my prayers. We're now living in a troubled time. Mark is dead. Giselle is dead, both killed by the unspeakable evil that is incarnated in the evil Stella. This disciple of the devil has tried to possess the souls of me and Oliver, and even my mother, Sarah, who, thanks to your miracle-working graces, is recovering in the hospital..."

Carmen paused and Oliver saw from the corner of his eye the white floral-patterned blinds gently twirl as a breeze swept in.

Carmen glanced at the fluttering blinds, locked eyes with Oliver again, and continued: "Oh, God Almighty, I summon you in our moment of torment and tragedy to bring your benevolent presence forth and banish Stella to the bowels of hell..."

The incoming wind intensified and the candle flames flickered. Goosebumps crawled up their arms.

Yet, Carmen, undeterred, continued with more passion and conviction: "Yes, Lord, banish her to hell and chain her up tightly so she never again returns to wreak havoc on the mortal world."

Carmen paused as a misty black substance swept into the room from the window and slowly swirled around.

She stiffened, gripped Oliver's hands tighter, and winked.

They closed their eyes and she continued: "I beg you, God, rid our lives of this evil forever. Use your power to release the evil presence threatening us..."

Carmen's prayer was abruptly interrupted by the gathering black mass. As it swirled around the room, it grew in size and intensified in force and fury.

Oliver felt Carmen's hands grip him even tighter.

"Don't open your eyes until I finish," she said.

"Okay," he said, shivering with the intensifying cold fury.

"In the name of the Father, the Son, and the Holy Ghost, leave us forever you evil bitch... amen," Carmen said.

"Amen," Oliver said, at which time they both opened their eyes.

The swirling black tornado descended upon them. In one fell swoop, it lifted the sacred book, along with three candles and Milton and Isabella, and smashed them into the wall. The table levitated and Carmen and Oliver steeled their elbows against it and steadied it back on the floor.

A voice, ominous, booming, and dripping with sarcasm: "You try, useless and weak humans, but you fail..."

"No!" Carmen shouted. "You fail... you will fail and God will win."

The chairs and table, Carmen and Oliver, flew into the air and twirled around the room violently.

"Noooooo." Oliver dove forward, hugging Carmen tightly. Still spinning, they drifted away from the table and chairs, joined by dolls and debris.

"God help us," Oliver said. "Please, God help us..."

The black tornado smashed them into a wall. Oliver landed on top of Carmen, bringing both hands up to shield them from falling debris. A table careened toward them and he blocked it with an arm. It bounced off his arm, flew into a wall, and splintered into pieces. A chair made an abrupt turn and flew at him, but he blocked it with a raised elbow and sent it spinning toward the open window. He watched it get sucked out and disappear.

He rolled off Carmen and propped her up against the wall beside him. They stared, shocked and horrified, watching as the swirling black magic mist separated into two beings, two long-haired, shadowy women to be sure.

The tornadic fury abruptly halted and the two women dropped to the debris-strewn floor, circling each other cautiously and preparing to square off.

***

Selina knew with dread certainty that this was her one and only chance to destroy her evil alter-ego, and she vowed with every fiber of her mysterious being that she was gonna do just that. Aided and abetted by Oliver and Carmen, the Lord God Almighty, and the sacred and enigmatic dolls, all the forces of good had culminated at this moment for one reason—to triumph over evil.

Selina circled her prey deftly, vying for an opening. As she saw Stella reach down for a chair leg, hoping to get a leg up in this epic battle, she seized the moment. She bent her head down and sprang forward, hitting Stella squarely in the chest and knocking her into the wall.

The chair leg flew out of her hand as Stella withered down the wall, groaning in pain but yet still grinning maniacally.

But Selina had every intention in the otherworld of wiping that grin from her face. She got up quickly, grabbed Stella by the ankles, and dragged her into the middle of the room. Once there, she mounted her and pummeled her repeatedly in the face.

As she watched Stella's face turn to blood-red pulp, Selina grinned. *Vengeance is mine. Finally, vengeance is mine.*

But it wouldn't be that easy. In one swift motion, Stella bucked furiously and Selina soared through the air, crashing into a wall head-first. Dazed, she felt a sharp pain in her head as she wilted down the wall, landing on her back, blood-dripping head propped up against the wall.

Stella leaped to her feet, picked up another table leg, and charged forward, plumes of fire spewing from her flared nostrils. "You die, once and for all, bitch."

"Fuck you," Selina said, the brain fog clearing enough to bring her foot up and kick Stella squarely between the legs.

Stella groaned and buckled and Selina sprang to her feet, guided by supernatural force and divine intervention. She picked up the table leg and smashed Stella repeatedly about the head and body.

Stella groaned, writhed, and screamed, but to no avail. Once unleashed, Selina's pent-up rage and fury knew no bounds.

Soon, Stella's body was a mass of bloody pulp. Finally, she stopped, stood over her prey victoriously, and grinned. "Who gets the last laugh now? Huh? Not you, that's for sure."

She wiped a few droplets of blood from her face, tossed the table leg haphazardly away, and stood back to admire her handiwork.

A gust of wind swept through the window, collected what remained of Stella into one small swirling black mass, and swept her out the window. Selina thought she heard a last painful cry of resignation from her evil twin but she couldn't be sure.

But she knew one thing for sure. Her work was done here. She turned around, looking down benevolently at Oliver and Carmen, both jaw-dropped and frozen with fear.

"She won't bother you anymore," Selina said. "I promise."

With that, her black shadowy image slowly transformed into a soft white glow. Then it floated up, curled into a spinning ball of energy, and soared out the window and far up into the heavens.

***

"Thank you, God," Carmen said, after they'd both somewhat recovered from the shock of it all.

"Amen," Oliver said, taking her by the hand and helping her to her feet.

Carmen embraced him in a tight hug, cradling her head on his shoulder as a tear slipped from her eye, rolled down her flushed cheek, and dropped onto his shoulder.

When they released, she loudly proclaimed, "We're cured!"

"I'd have to agree," Oliver said, rushing over to the window and gazing at the sky, looking for a remnant, any remnant of Selina. But all he saw were a few twinkling stars, mostly washed out by city lights, and the full and ominously glowing moon. He closed the window, pulled the blinds tightly shut, and surveyed the room

Carmen had already moved over to where Isabella had landed. She was pinned under some debris in a corner of the room. She pushed the debris away, picked up the doll, and frowned. "She's got a crack in the back of her head."

"Shit, that sucks," Oliver said, noticing the pant leg of Milton sticking out from underneath the tabletop. He rushed over, lifted the table, and picked up Milton. The doll had a long crack on his forehead that snaked down the side of his nose and onto his cheek, stopping about an inch from his wide and friendly grin.

"Milton's injured as well."

After their hearts had returned to beating with a rhythm that approximated normal, they organized a clean-up plan and soon Oliver was busy sweeping the room, picking up the pieces of the China dolls and placing them carefully on the dresser, which had remarkably been spared by the gale-force winds created by the malicious tornado. He'd also fetched three plastic utility bins and now had most of the wood bits from the shattered table and chairs stuffed inside.

Carmen busied herself gluing a chunk of plastic (or glass, Oliver didn't know) on the back of Isabella's head. When she had finished, she carefully applied a line of glue to Milton's injury and placed him lovingly beside Isabella, behind the shattered remains of the China dolls.

Oliver watched her set Milton down next to Isabella and picked up the table top. "Where do you want this?"

"Put it outside next to the garbage," she said. "Near the alley."

Twenty minutes later, they had the ritual room spic and span, and they stood at the door admiring their work. Even the sacred book had survived the ordeal and was now safely tucked between Milton and Isabella.

"I don't think we need them anymore, do you?" Carmen said, pointing to the dolls.

Oliver shook his head.

"I'll buy some glue tomorrow on the way home from the nursing home," Carmen said, closing the door. "For the China dolls."

***

With Carmen sleeping peacefully by his side, Oliver watched the flickering candle flame paint dancing yellow lines across the ceiling and wall. At one point, a yellow monster appeared to rise up, his garish grin enveloping the ceiling. Oliver closed his eyes and reopened them confidently and the monster was gone.

After a deliciously slow and tantalizing lovemaking session with Carmen, he now felt sure all the demons had been exorcised. This was no longer the calm before the storm. It was the calm after the storm. It was peace of mind, tranquility, and the beginning of a powerful bond with the real love of his life, one Carmen Weathersby.

He sighed and moved closer to Carmen, spooning her and smiling. He knew whatever obstacles they now faced would pale in comparison to what they'd been through. And their struggles had armed them with a new-and-improved toughness and resiliency that would help them beat all odds. Not only survive, but thrive.

"Thank you, God," he said, closing his eyes and drifting off into a deep, dreamless, and rejuvenating sleep.

Chapter Twenty-Four

Last night's calm and confidence was gone with the wind.

"I don't know what my reservations are, but it just doesn't feel right," Oliver said, as they pulled into the parking lot of King's Garden.

Carmen parked, turned off the ignition, and they studied the building. A tall red brick structure that seemed to have eyes for windows, it stood on a grassy hill, the parking lot a good 200 feet from the main entrance. It resembled something out of a haunted insane asylum movie. Black, high pitched roof. Dark wooden window shutters, some mysteriously closed. Large oak trees dotted the path leading up the hill, barren of greenery, their prickly branches angrily overhanging the trail. Even the lawn had strange dark patches every ten or so feet. Behind and above the aged-looking facility, a bank of clouds moved toward them, slowing obscuring the crimson-colored setting sun.

A few of the lights dotting the entrance pathway, mounted on decorative steel poles, flickered. Two of them winked out.

"Well, if we're gonna check it out, we better get going," Carmen said. "It's getting dark. And, look... some of those lights are going out."

"That's not a good sign," Oliver said, beads of sweat beginning to crawl down his forehead.

Carmen tugged at his arm. "Come on, honey. Let's get this over with."

Carmen had to practically drag Oliver to the entrance. They arrived at a pair of large and ornate, bright red steel doors.

"It's closed," Oliver said. "Let's go home."

"Look," Carmen said, pointing to a key-pad, incongruously modern. She leaned forward and pressed a series of buttons. A large buzzing sound echoed through the dark and tree-lined property.

Both doors opened inward with a mechanical squeak.

Oliver puzzled over how Carmen knew the entry code. *She must've got it when she booked the appointment, silly.*

Carmen and Oliver stepped back.

Standing in the brightly lit entrance hallway was a crotchety-looking old lady with a cane and a neatly pressed gray uniform. A white plastic name tag pinned to her hollow chest read: *Sybil Rasmussen, Administrator.*

Two tall and muscular-looking orderlies with bald heads stood at her side grinning broadly, both dressed in neatly pressed and starched white uniforms.

Oliver almost turned and fled, but Carmen grabbed his arm, yanking him forward with ferocious force.

"It's gonna be okay," Carmen whispered. "Everything's gonna be okay."

"Welcome," Sybil said in a raspy voice, grinning and exposing dark holes between her crooked yellow teeth. "I'm the administrator." The wrinkles lining her face widened, darkened, and snaked along her sunken cheeks.

She raised her black cane. "You must be Carmen." The cane moved to Oliver. "And you must be Oliver. Come in. We've been expecting you."

Wiping a sweaty brow and trying desperately to still a struggling heartbeat, Oliver stepped forward. Carmen had grabbed his hand, a human security blanket in a macabre and surreal scene that resembled one of his horror flicks.

As they stepped into the foyer, white, clean and sterile-looking despite the monstrous exterior of the facility, the administrator led them over to a sign-in book, where she handed them an old-fashioned ink pen and instructed them to sign in.

The orderlies loomed behind them, silent but deadly-looking.

"You're gonna love this facility," Sybil said. "Follow me."

She led them down a long and winding hallway, extolling the virtues of King's Garden. The orderlies followed close behind. Oliver only half-listened as his mind got distracted by other incongruities. All of the doors to all of the rooms were closed. They passed one room with a glass window. A wild-eyed man imprisoned in a straitjacket pounded his head into the reinforced glass, each blow creating a fresh splatter of blood. "Let me outta here!"

Carmen didn't seem to notice. If she did notice, she evidently didn't care.

"What's with him," Oliver said, interrupting Sybil's monologue.

She waved a hand dismissively. "Oh, that's just Walter. Don't worry about him. He won't hurt you. He's stark-raving mad, but he can't escape."

Oliver stopped. "I don't think... I don't think this place is the right fit for your mother."

Carmen reassured him soothingly. "It's okay, honey. Let's at least see the facilities."

In spite of his strong reservations and racing heart, Oliver continued.

"At King's Garden, we pride ourselves in resident care and health," Sybil said. "We have a hairdresser, podiatrist, many on-site specialists. We have a gymnasium, a lounge area, a bingo hall, and even a weekly pub night every Thursday in the basement. Our institution celebrates living by providing quality care."

Reaching the end of a long white corridor, shadowed closely by the orderlies, they arrived at a cafeteria, where they stopped and peered through the large glass-paned windows. About a hundred residents sat around a cluster of tables. Some slurped up squirming worms. One man hacked into a blood-soaked hand with a hatchet, and as he chopped off the fingers, he stuffed them into his mouth ravenously. Another man picked at a human brain delicately with a fork and knife.

At the sight of the brain-eating man, Oliver felt his stomach lurch. Then the man sawed off a neat slice of brain with the serrated edged knife, and held it up with a broad grin as brain matter dribbled down his cheek.

"This is fucking crazy," Oliver said trying to move but unable to. His feet were frozen in fear to the spot.

"It's pretty far from fucking crazy," Sybil said with a cheery smile. "All of our residents eat nutritionally balanced meals three times a day. In between, they even get snacks delivered to their rooms. Tea, coffee, some cookies, or fruit maybe."

Oliver tugged at Carmen's sleeve. "Do you see what I see?"

"I see nutritionally balanced meals, as Sybil says." Carmen dismissed Oliver with a wave and turned to Sybil. "Impressive. Impressive indeed. I think my mom will like it here."

"I'm sure she'll like it here," Sybil said. "The foundation of our care is built on recognizing each resident's past experiences, past friendships, and individual needs. We strive to foster a sense of well-being and belonging."

"You must be outta your mind," Oliver said, tugging Carmen's sleeve with adrenaline-fueled force. "Don't you see what's happening? They're eating... they're eating people."

Carmen's mouth dropped open, eyes narrowing and face blanching as white as the institution walls.

"What are we doing?" she said, grabbing Oliver's hand, pulling him out of his horror-induced catatonia. "Let's go."

"Nonsense," Sybil said. "Nothing...and I mean nothing could be further from the truth."

Both orderlies moved to grab Oliver and Carmen, but they had already gotten a good head start, both fleeing down the hall hand in hand. They rounded a corner and stopped, panting for breath, both realizing the orderlies were gaining on them.

No time to breathe.

"Look," Oliver said, pointing to a red neon EXIT sign that appeared to materialize out of thin air.

They sprinted toward it, stopped and pulled open the door. There were stairs leading down to a dark and cavernous abyss.

"I don't know," Oliver said. "It looks scary."

"Not like we have a choice," Carmen said, grabbing his arm. "Maybe there's an escape tunnel."

Hearing the thumping of footsteps behind them, they descended the spiral metal staircase, finally reaching the bottom and looking around. It was a rock tunnel with a slimy, black ooze-soaked floor. It was lit every thirty or so feet by dangling red incandescent lights. Wasting little time, they slogged through the ooze. About a minute later, they reached a six-pronged fork in the eerie road and stopped.

"Which way?" Oliver asked, between breaths.

Carmen counted from left to right, stopping at tunnel number three. "This one."

They proceeded up a rock staircase and into the pitch-black tunnel. Feeling their way along the walls, Oliver felt a cold metal handle. "A door. In here."

Now it was Oliver pulling Carmen inside, closing the door behind them and pinning his formidable mass behind the door as Carmen sat down to catch her breath. The rock-walled room was lit by a single yellow light that dangled from the ceiling—back and forth, back and forth, back and forth.

Oliver could see nothing else in the room. No furniture, nothing.

The thumping footfalls grew louder.

"Hold your breath," Oliver whispered. "I can hear them."

Finding energy reserves they didn't know they had, they inhaled deeply and held their breaths.

They heard the nearing footfalls. *Thump, thump, thump thump thump thump.*

And, somewhere off in the distance, incessant and maddening water droplets.

Drip, drop, drip, drop, drip, drop drip drop drip drop.

The footfalls stopped, right outside the door. "Are you in there?" a gruff male voice asked.

They stayed silent and waited. It seemed like hours but Oliver knew it was probably only seconds.

Drip, drop, drip, drop, drip, drop drip drop drip drop.

And then the footfalls started again, slowly fading away. The sound vanished entirely and only then did they both exhale long and desperate breaths.

"That was a close call," Oliver said finally.

"It sure was," Carmen agreed. "We gotta find a way outta here."

They moved around the room, touching the damp walls. Oliver heard the sound of shifting dirt.

"Over here," Carmen said.

Oliver spun around and saw that she had somehow managed to pull a large boulder out of the wall, revealing another tunnel about three feet in diameter. He watched her bend down and crawl inside.

Her hollow voice echoed into the dungeon-like chamber. "Let's go. We don't have much time."

"Be right there," Oliver said. He went over to the steel door, feeling the edges and found what he was looking for—a steel barrel bolt lock. He tugged on it and with some effort managed to release it from its rusty home and slide it into place, locking the door.

As he crawled inside the small tunnel, he heard the footfalls return, followed by pounding on the door. A booming authoritative voice said, "You can run but you can't hide."

As Carmen and Oliver crawled through the damp and smelly tunnel, the pounding on the door faded, along with the male voice commanding them to open the door.

After ten or so minutes, the tunnel sloped downward and they found themselves sliding helplessly on slimy ooze for a few seconds before dropping to the ground. Oliver landed ass-first, wincing as a bolt of pain shot up his tailbone. But he had the foresight to look up and extend his arms, catching Carmen with both hands as she dropped from above.

He felt her pillowy-soft butt cheeks scrunch into his face and they rolled over a couple of times before coming to a stop on a wet concrete surface.

Oliver took stock of their new surroundings. It was an oval-shaped hallway with a series of leaking pipes running along the ceiling. It was lit by wall-mounted fluorescent lights, spaced about fifteen to twenty feet apart. About an inch of water and mud covered the floor.

Oliver got up, helping Carmen to her feet, examining her to make sure she was okay. Her jeans were mostly soaking wet and caked with mud. Her hair was matted to her mud-streaked face and a few buttons on her long-sleeved V-neck blouse had popped open, revealing ample cleavage. Instinctively, he reached over and buttoned up her shirt, stepping back to evaluate her a second time.

"Thanks for breaking my fall, and dressing me," she said. "Are you okay?"

Oliver looked himself over. There was a tear in the knee of his jeans and his kneecap was caked with blood and mud. His once oversized white T-shirt was covered with large brown splatter marks and, judging from the putrid smell, he surmised it was a mixture of shit and mud, perhaps more shit than mud.

He wiped his face with a hand, realizing it too was splotched with mud and, yes, probably shit stains. "I'm gonna have to be okay. We need to find a way outta here still."

Carmen pinched her nostrils and pointed at the trickling water. "It stinks like sewage in here. I say we follow the creek."

"Shit creek without a paddle."

They burst into uproarious laughter tinged with a hint of mania. Finally, they stopped laughing and started walking, Oliver taking the lead.

"What do you think that was all about back there?" Oliver asked as they moved down the tunnel.

"Madness," Carmen said, her voice echoing eerily off the corridor walls.

"What?"

"Everyone around us is going crazy."

"That place isn't a nursing home," Oliver said. "It's a nuthouse."

"That it is," Carmen said. "And we're gonna get as far away from it as possible."

"I don't understand. I mean, the pictures on the internet looked much different than the actual building. How can that be possible?"

"After everything we've been through," Carmen said, "believe me, anything's possible. Everything's possible."

Oliver swallowed a rising lump in his throat, a neat little mucous-wrapped ball of fear, paranoia, and confusion. As much as he wanted to make sense of it, he just couldn't. They rounded a corner and stopped for a moment, examining the long, straight passageway ahead. At its end, which appeared to be about a mile away, it was brightly lit with a warm yellow glow, in stark contrast to the blinding white fluorescent lights.

"Look," Oliver said. "A light at the end of the tunnel."

They looked at each other in amusement for a split-second. Two grins spread across two faces and more laughter followed. When the loud and creepily echoing mirth finally subsided, Carmen said, "So cliché and so hilarious."

"Yeah," Oliver said. "But we better get moving and start taking this seriously."

Carmen gave him a serious look and they carried on.

They stopped for a break, Oliver leaning on one side of the wall, Carmen facing him on the other.

"We're almost..." A black streak barreling toward them caught his eye. They stood stalk-still and watched as the streak grew into a menacingly large and slimy alligator-like creature, hundreds of oversized and razor-sharp fangs snapping hungrily as it rocketed toward them.

"Oh shit," Oliver said, snapping into fight-over-flight mode. He scanned the muddy floor and quickly spotted the object of his desire—a long metal pipe. He picked it up, telling Carmen to "back off" while he steadied himself at home plate and positioned the improvised bat to strike.

With blinding speed, the creature reached them. Oliver swung the bat with incredible force and precisely at the right time, striking the creature and tearing off its elongated lower jaw. It smashed into the wall. As it slithered down, Oliver leaped forward and pounded the creature in the head a second, third, fourth, fifth, sixth, and seventh time—seventh heaven—watching it wriggly, squirm, squeal and eventually grow quiet and still.

Oliver raised the bloody pipe triumphantly. "All in a day's work."

"Home run," Carmen said. "You're my hero."

"I guess I am," Oliver said, wiping a few drops of blood from his face and kissing Carmen on the cheek. "We better get going while we still can."

But as soon as they turned and took one step forward, another creature emerged, identical to the last, propelling itself toward them with supernatural speed.

Oliver's fearless and heroic home run ignited Carmen's fury. "Gimme that bat and step back," she said. "It's my turn."

Oliver complied.

Carmen stepped up to the plate, crouched down and readied the improvised bat. "Come and meet your maker, mother fucker."

The creature did and she finished it off in almost exactly the same fashion as Oliver had. When she'd finished, she spun around, wiped a drop of blood from her lips, and kissed Oliver on the cheek.

He had just emerged from a defensive posture—shifting rapidly from fearlessness to fearfulness and back to fearlessness again as another creature bit the dust.

"Home run," Oliver said. "Home team two, evil team zero."

"We're exorcising our demons," Carmen said triumphantly. "That's what this is all about."

With renewed purpose and finally an understanding of their mission, they continued on, alternating stops along the way to switch batting positions and pound creatures to pulp.

Finally, they arrived at the light at the end of the tunnel, covered with blood, guts, and gore, and whatever sewage matter splatter they'd picked up along the way.

"I feel super-charged," Carmen said, tossing the lead pipe aside and peering up a metal ladder leading to the glowing yellow light.

"You look like hell," Oliver said. "But at least we've arrived at the light at the end of the tunnel." He bowed ceremoniously and gestured with a wave of his hand and Carmen grinned and started her ascent.

"Oh, thank you, Lord," she said when she reached the surface and climbed out.

"What's up there?" Oliver asked.

"It's heaven," she said gleefully. "Pure heaven."

Oliver couldn't believe his eyes when he arrived at the surface. They were in an ornate ballroom of an ancient castle. There was a water fountain in the middle of the room with a naked bow-and-arrow-armed cupid atop a large tower in the center of it, water spraying in all directions and cascading down into the surrounding circular fountain walls. Around the room, vibrantly colored plush sofas and chairs were strewn about. On the tables and chairs, some even spread out on intricately woven and richly textured carpets, were men and women in various stages of lovemaking—an orgy of monumental proportion. Strategically placed ornate tables were heaped with drink and food, some occupied by couples lovingly feeding each other, feasting on the culinary delights, feasting on each other's naked bodies. Soft exotic Egyptian music seeped into the room.

"Yippee," Carmen said gleefully. She peeled off her clothes, leaped into the fountain, and began washing herself in the cascading water.

"It's warm and delicious," she said. "Come on in."

Oliver didn't waste any time, stripping off his clothes and diving into the cascading water with a loud belly-flop splash.

Carmen had miraculously located a bar of soap and was busy massaging a rich foamy lather into her voluptuous breasts, kneading them tenderly and beginning to moan softly.

Don't think, just do. Don't think, just do. Too afraid that if he opened and closed his eyes too many times, or even pinched himself, he would wake up in his dreary apartment, look at the clock, and realize it was time to go to his stupid customer service job. So he just acted instinctively, following the lead of his swollen member. After dunking his head in the warm and soothing water, he rushed into Carmen's arms, marveling at how her large breasts and erect nipples felt pressing against his chest.

"I don't know how we did it, but we're in heaven," Oliver said.

"Never mind how," Carmen said. "Just enjoy the moment."

Another bar of soap appeared and Oliver grabbed it, scrubbing himself, scrubbing Carmen, scrubbing himself again. When they were lickety-split clean, the lovemaking began.

Barely able to contain his sexual appetite, Oliver kissed Carmen long and passionately, letting his hands roam freely to her erogenous zones. She moaned with pleasure at his touch and reciprocated by finding his swollen member and stroking it gently and slowly.

After a few minutes of foreplay, Oliver was getting close to exploding and wanted to dry off and make love in a more comfortable position on one of those plush throw rugs somewhere.

"Follow me," he said, taking her hand and guiding her out of the fountain. A gleaming metal towel rack magically appeared and Oliver grabbed two bright red towels, handing one to Carmen, and drying himself off.

When they were good and dry, he plucked a burgundy robe off the rack, draped it over Carmen, and took another matching robe for himself. Then he led Carmen through the ball room, moans of orgiastic pleasure echoing all around them. He spotted a gleaming silver door in a nearby hallway and opened it. It was just as he thought—richly adorned with expensive carpets hanging from all four walls; a king-size four-poster bed in the corner; candle lights adorning every corner of the dark red room.

As soon as he closed the door, Carmen slipped her robe off and rushed into his arms, landing on top of him on the bed. He moaned, not with pain but with a deep and satisfying pleasure. Carmen's expert hand found his dick and slipped it into her dripping wet pussy.

Both of them moaning in perfect synchronicity, Carmen began a slow thrust that gradually became faster and more frenetic until both of them came simultaneously, Carmen screaming with delight and Oliver moaning loudly.

After their breathing had normalized, Carmen planted a wet kiss on Oliver's lips and hugged him tightly.

In less than two minutes, they drifted off to sleep, hugging each other tightly.

Chapter Twenty-Five

"Where am I?" Oliver said, slowly opening his eyes.

There was no response from Carmen, who was sleeping peacefully next to him.

He climbed out of bed, careful not to wake sleeping beauty, and surveyed his surroundings. A sterile white utilitarian room. A closet in one corner, the door slightly ajar. A nightstand on one side of the bed, standard institutional issue. *What?* A large orange vinyl-covered armchair next to the bed, which, after locating and pulling on his underwear and T-shirt, he plopped himself into.

Oliver's mind swam with indistinct images of the recent narrow escape from the nursing home; the brutal exorcism of demons; the frenzied sexual ecstasy that followed, and the cozy and ornate bedroom where he'd finally fallen asleep.

With widening eyes, he scanned the room again, confusion and fear etched in his brow. "Where the hell am I?"

He saw a window, the blinds fluttering as a gentle breeze swept into the room. He approached it, spread the blinds, and looked outside. It was a bright sunny day and the expansive grounds were neatly manicured and dotted with large oak and maple trees, many of which had benches or picnic tables underneath. People—patients?—wearing drab gray uniforms were below, some strolling, others sitting, still others engaged in animated conversation. In the distance, he saw a steel black fence bordering the property, its spiked fence posts sending an emphatic message of forced containment.

"Carmen," he said, stifling the urge to drop to his knees and start crying. "Wake up. Something's gone wrong. We gotta get outta here."

Carmen stirred but didn't wake up.

The door burst open and Oliver backed into the window, afraid that one of the monsters he'd beaten to a pulp last night had been resurrected from the grave and was coming for revenge.

A bald man in a white lab coat entered, followed by two bald orderlies. Oliver recognized them instantly as the men from last night who had pursued them. But this man in the middle, monkey in the middle, who was he? A doctor. Looked like one. Where had Oliver seen him before?"

The orderlies moved toward Oliver and stopped a few feet away.

"Oliver, how many times have I told you? You can't sneak into Carmen's room and spend the night. That's not allowed in this facility."

Carmen stirred and bolted up in bed, her eyes popping out of her head at the sight of the three men.

Oliver fought an urge to spin around and crash through the window and drop five floors to his death. His world had been turned upside down in a matter of days and now it appeared he was... he couldn't bring himself to say it. He tried to calm himself down. If they were to make their escape, they had to play it safe and act normal. A flash of recognition struck him. The man. Doctor Stevens. He'd seen him at the hospital where Carmen's mother was still recovering. Even then he'd struck Oliver as odd and had said some weird things.

"I'm sorry, doctor," Oliver said. "It won't happen again."

Doctor Stevens raised an eyebrow. "Are you sure? Are you sure you even know where you are?"

"I know where we are," Carmen said, leaping out of bed, realizing she was naked, and covering herself with a blanket as her eyes frantically searched the floor for her clothes. She spotted an oversized white T-shirt, bent down, and picked it up, throwing the blanket aside and giving all spectators a split-second view of her nakedness before she pulled the garment on and backed into the wall as the orderlies approached her.

"Where are we, Carmen?" Doctor Stevens asked.

She pointed to the approaching orderlies. "Don't let them near me! We're in the Toronto General Hospital. You've... you've finally captured us."

Doctor Stevens produced a syringe, squirted a tiny stream of clear liquid into the air, and advanced.

Oliver watched the scene unfold, horrified. "Leave her alone!"

"You stay outta this," an orderly scowled, "or you'll get sedated too."

Another orderly entered the room, a behemoth of a man almost seven feet tall, and quickly moved toward Oliver with a raised finger, stopping within six inches of his face and staring down at him with an unmistakable message: Make a move and you'll pay dearly.

The orderlies moved in, grabbed Carmen, and pushed her on the bed, pinning her down by her arms as she kicked, screamed, and yelled obscenities. Finally one of them got her arm tied off and Doctor Stevens moved in closer with the syringe.

"It saddens me to think that our little experiment didn't work," he said. "We let you guys play out your little fantasy hoping that it would bring you back to the real world, but unfortunately, I don't believe it has. We'll have to start a new type of treatment I'm afraid—one that's far more aggressive."

The doctor bent down and injected Carmen with the syringe. Her frantic screaming and struggling stopped and she collapsed in a heap on the bed. The orderlies stepped back, admiring their handiwork.

Fucking assholes, Oliver thought, narrowing his eyes. *Carmen's right. Somehow they captured us and are feeding us a line of shit. Brainwashing us. But go along with them, or you're fucked.* "The experiment *did* work, Doctor Stevens. I'm cured."

The mammoth orderly applied a vice-like grip to his shoulder and sneered at him.

Oliver winced and shrank.

"Not too rough, Bruce," the doctor said, approaching Oliver. "These are patients and I'm trying to cure them."

Bruce loosened his grip a little, but not a lot.

"You're cured?" the doctor asked, nearing.

A nurse wheeled a stretcher into the room and parked it beside Carmen's bed. The two orderlies lifted her onto it and strapped her in.

Oliver watched and wondered. Could he smash this man's steel grip, spin around, and crash through the window. *No, gotta save Carmen.* "Where are they taking her?"

"Don't you worry about your new girlfriend," the doctor said. "She's in good hands. I promise. Now, don't distract me. I know how good you are at distraction. You say you're cured?"

"Yes... I'm... I'm cured," Oliver stammered.

"Then where are we?"

Oliver opened his mouth to speak and closed it again, wracking his brain for a suitable answer. "We're in some kind of a hospital."

"That's obvious. What hospital?"

He shrank to his knees and looked up at the doctor as a wave of sadness washed over him. "I... I don't know."

Bruce bent down and pulled Oliver to his feet. Oliver didn't resist. He was defeated, deflated, devastated, and depressed as he watched the orderlies wheel Carmen out of the room.

"Now, let's get you back to your room now," Doctor Stevens said. "We'll talk later."

Chapter Twenty-Six

Carmen opened her eyes, slowly measuring her surroundings. A white padded room with a white padded door and a small window. A single bed. A nightstand. A table and two chairs in the middle of the room. Her head ached dully and she squirmed in an effort to rub her temple. But she couldn't move. She was wrapped tightly in a straitjacket. She noticed her legs were unbound and, with some effort, managed to seat herself at the foot of the bed.

A million thoughts and a million images assaulted her senses, most of them disjointed and non-sequential. What had gone wrong? One day she and Oliver had been possessed by a demon, the next day they'd exorcised the demon. One day they didn't know each other, the next day they not only knew each other but they were madly in love. One day her mother was at home, the next day she'd been attacked by a demon and had wound up in the Toronto General Hospital. One day her brother and sister were alive and well, the next day they were dead, brutally murdered by the demon. *Really? Who really killed them?* One day she was working as a secretary, the next she was battling evil and living with Oliver in her mother's modest abode. One day they were checking out a nursing home for Mom, the next they were in an institute of horror and being chased by murderous orderlies. One minute they were beating monsters to a pulp with lead pipes, the next minute they were making wild and passionate love in a richly textured and romantic room in a castle of sexual pleasure; only to wake up and find herself here in a straitjacket in a white padded room and, what, batshit crazy? *But, no, it couldn't be. Or could it?*

How much of it was real? Was her whole life a dream? A nightmare? Was it a metaphor for madness?

A tear formed on her eyelid as sadness and despair swept over her. She closed her eyes and released the tear. Soon it was joined by another one. She slumped her head on her bosom and let the grief flow. What choice did she have?

She heard the metallic click of a deadbolt lock sliding open, followed by a short, sharp squeak. The padded door opened and a bald man in a white lab coat entered the room. He held a file in one hand, a pen in the other. Two orderlies accompanied him. One closed the door while the other followed the doctor as he approached the bed.

"I'm sorry to see you crying, Carmen. I understand this must be difficult for you."

She recognized the man. Doctor Stevens. But he was supposed to be her mother's physician at Toronto General Hospital. Not her doctor at some... at some... nuthouse.

"Are you... are you here to help me?" she asked, the fight rapidly draining from her. It's not like she had a lot to fight about right now given her restrained condition.

The doctor sat down at the table in the middle of the room. "I've always been here to help you."

She licked her lips, feeling the salty taste of teardrops. She struggled to wipe her eyes, but the straitjacket wouldn't allow it.

"I'd like to ask you some questions," Doctor Stevens said. "If I take that off will you cooperate with me?"

"Yes."

"You won't get violent?"

"Do I get violent?"

"Sometimes."

"I won't hurt you. I won't get violent. I promise."

"Will you answer my questions as honestly as you can?"

"Sure. I have a lot of questions of my own."

"I'm sure you do. And, if we have time, maybe we'll get to some of your questions today."

"Thanks," Carmen said weakly.

Doctor Stevens nodded to the orderlies. They removed her straitjacket, led her over to the table, and sat her down.

"You can go," the doctor said to the orderlies. "Tell Nurse Karen Ramsey to bring in a Diet Coke and some Kleenex, will you?"

The orderlies nodded and left.

Carmen wiped her tears away and pushed back her hair, a clump of which had fallen over her eyes.

"Let's wait a minute, shall we? Are you thirsty?"

Carmen nodded.

"How are you feeling?"

"Tired. Drowsy."

"That's the sedative. It'll wear off in a few hours."

"Where's Oliver?"

Before the doctor could answer, Nurse Ramsey entered the room. "Here we go," she said, putting a box of Kleenex on the table and handing Carmen a can of Diet Coke.

"Thanks," Carmen said.

The nurse walked away and stopped at the door. "Do you want this closed?"

"Please," Carmen said, thinking the woman looked more like a librarian than a nurse, especially with the black-framed glasses.

She left the room, closing the door behind her.

Carmen popped the tab on the soft drink and took a long sip, instant relief for her dry and parched throat. Then she took three tissues, wiped her eyes, blew her nose, scrunched the tissue, and inserted it into a pocket of her white pants.

"Sorry," she said.

"No need to apologize," Doctor Stevens said. "You were thirsty and you needed to wipe your eyes and blow your nose. All perfectly normal human functions."

He opened a file, flipped a few pages ahead, and made a notation. "Now, are you ready to get started?"

"Yes... how long have I been here? In isolation?"

"I'm supposed to be the one asking questions, but I'll answer that. After you had your... your most recent nervous breakdown, two weeks ago, we brought you here."

Two weeks of brain fog. Holy shit. It's only gonna get worse from here. "Thanks."

Doctor Stevens referenced his file. "Now, do you know where you are?"

The Toronto General Hospital didn't work last time. "No."

"You're at the Mississauga Psychiatric Institute."

Carmen's mouth dropped open. "A nuthouse?"

"We don't like to use that term around here. Do you know how long you've been here?"

"Two weeks?"

"You've been two weeks in isolation. You've been at this institute for five years."

"Oh my God! How did I wind up here?"

"We'll get to that in a minute. As part of a ground-breaking new psychiatric treatment, we at the institute conducted a little experiment. We decided to let you and Oliver play out your little fantasy in the hope that it might help you identify your demons, come to grips with them, and exorcise them. I think it succeeded in part, but I'm afraid in large part it failed. It not only failed but it started getting a little unmanageable. Does the name Stella mean anything to you?"

"Stella was a demon. But she's been banished to hell now. She's gone."

"I'm glad she's gone," the doctor said. "That's the good news. Stella was actually one of your multiple personalities that you constructed to hide the tragedy and repress your pain. She was a coping mechanism and a convenient scapegoat to lay the blame on."

"But I saw her."

"Of course you did. Delusional and hallucinatory multiple personality disorder causes sufferers to see all kinds of things. She was never real, though. Only in your minds. Now, let's move on. Does the name Selina mean anything to you?"

"Selina was Stella's alter-ego. She was her angelic side. You know, the good side."

"And where is Selina now?"

"She's in heaven. She beat the crap out of Stella and then soared up to heaven. She saved our lives."

"That's good to hear," Doctor Stevens said, taking notes. "That she's no longer one of your multiple personalities. And I'm glad you know you're Carmen."

"Of course I do. How many personalities do I... did I have?"

The doctor referred to his file. "From what we've learned by letting you and Oliver play out your fantasy world, let me see. Giselle had a bit part. Mark had a bit part. Ruby and Finley, minor parts. Patricia, small role. A Detective Stanley Darby, significant, but still a bit part. Sarah, a larger role. And of course Stella and Selina, much larger roles. To my math, that's nine. I might be wrong, but I don't think so."

The magnitude of Carmen's psychosis smashed her in the head like a lead pipe. She dropped her head in her hands and had to fight to hold back the tears. This new information begged several questions, many of which she was too afraid to ask.

"Take some time to compose yourself," Doctor Stevens said. "We can take a break if you want. We can continue another day."

"No. If I'm gonna get better I need to know everything."

"Well, that much is true," Doctor Stevens said. "Do you think you're ready for the whole story?"

"If I'm not, you can leave me to suffer in isolation when you're done. You're probably gonna do that anyway."

"We won't release you into the general patient population until we're sure you're ready. And I don't think you are right now. But if you want to hear the story I'll tell it to you. It'll be the same story that I've told you many times before."

"Okay," Carmen whispered. "Please, enlighten me."

"Your father, Matheson, died of heart failure related to liver damage from alcoholism. You were only two years old at the time. Do you remember that?"

She did remember. Her mother had told her the truth not so long ago. "Yes."

She braced herself for the rest, hoping against all hope that she hadn't killed Mark, Giselle, or her mother, Sarah. Maybe they were still alive?

"In one of your moments of lucidity"—Doctor Stevens checked his file—"I told you three months ago what really happened to your father."

"My mother told me," Carmen said.

"No, Carmen. I'm afraid I did. Now, do you want to hear the rest?"

She nodded slowly, a lead ball of doom and gloom settling over her.

Doctor Stevens paused briefly, scrutinizing her readiness for the news. "Five and a half years ago, during a family Easter dinner get-together, your mother, brother, and sister died in a house fire. Investigators were never really able to piece together what happened. It was ruled an accident, but you blamed yourself. You escaped the fire, strangely, with three dolls you call Milton, Grace, and Isabella. Do you remember that night?"

Carmen wiped tear-filled eyes. "No. I thought Stella killed Giselle, Mark, and his girlfriend, Patricia. I thought my mother was alive and in Toronto General Hospital."

"I'm afraid your mother is dead. And if you're saying that Stella killed Giselle and Mark, and Stella is... err was one of your personalities, then maybe you killed Giselle and Mark. And, by definition, that means you killed your mother as well."

"I didn't kill them," Carmen said adamantly. "I didn't kill them!"

"But you don't really know that, do you? You blocked it all out, repressed it, and constructed this elaborate and complex fantasy world to cope with it and escape from it at the same time."

"I hope it comes to me," Carmen said. "I wanna know that I'm not evil."

"It might have been an accident," Doctor Stevens said. "Probably was an accident. But your overwhelming guilt and sadness led you into psychosis—acute hallucinatory multiple personality disorder."

"Maybe I'll remember. I hope I do remember."

"Well, that's part of what I've been trying to help you with all these years. But I'm afraid my little experiment can only be called a partial success at this stage. Let's see what the future brings."

"What about the dolls?"

"What about them?"

"Are they real?"

"Well, yes, they're real, but they're dolls."

"Where are they?"

"We have them in a safe place, and we'll return them to you when we return you to the general patient population, which I hope is sooner rather than later. The last time we tried taking them away from you, you went into a violent state of hysteria so we know better than to destroy them. Trust me, they're yours and they'll be returned to you."

"What role do they play in all of this?"

"You probably know the answer to that question better than I do. To the best of my understanding, they act as security blankets for you. They're your imagined protection against perceived evil. You've constructed a complicated world and I have to admit I'm only now starting to understand certain aspects of it."

"They were my mother's dolls at one time. Is that right?"

"That's what you've told us. Listen, I think we've done enough for one day." The doctor stood. "Thank you for cooperating with me. Maybe we've gone some way to making you better. Your dinner will be served soon. If we leave the straitjacket off, you won't hurt yourself or anyone else, right?"

"I promise."

"Are you sure?"

"Cross my heart."

"Okay. Nurse Ramsey will be here in an hour with your dinner. After dinner, she'll give you a sedative if you like. To my surprise, you've actually made a lot of progress today. But you've been bombarded with information overload and you may want something to calm you down. What do you think?"

Carmen was getting lambasted by multiple emotions—sadness, shock, a nagging and pervasive feeling of guilt that she may have killed her family, on purpose, or by accident. "I think I'll take the sedative."

He was at the door now. "I think that's a good idea."

Carmen stood up on jittery legs. She definitely needed some time alone to process all of this. She missed Oliver and wanted him to hold her tightly, comfort her with soothing words, and make it all go away. *But wait. Is he even real?*

"What about Oliver?" she asked.

"What about him?"

"Is he real?"

"Oh, he's real all right. He's been a patient here for over ten years and we've watched the two of you slowly but surely become attracted to each other. Unfortunately for him, he bought into your fantasy world and it became his fantasy world. But, please, Carmen, get some rest now."

"Will I get to see him again?"

"I don't know. Maybe."

Chapter Twenty-Seven

"Do you know where you are?" Doctor Stevens asked Oliver. He was sitting at his desk, backdropped by several neatly arranged filing cabinets.

Oliver sat across from him cross-legged, fidgeting nervously. "I'm in the Mississauga Psychiatric Institute."

The doctor arched his brow. "When we got you back to your room yesterday, you probably asked one of the patients. Would that be accurate?"

Oliver considered bluffing. But he had a sense Doctor Stevens would call a bluff. If he wanted to get out of here, if he wanted to see Carmen again, he better play ball. "Harvey, across the hall from me, told me."

Doctor Stevens opened his file, scribbled something, and eyed Oliver. "I thought so. And I appreciate your honesty."

"I hope you can shed some light on this," Oliver said. "Because right now I can't make any sense out of it."

"Do you remember how long you've been here?"

"We arrived yesterday morning."

"No. Yesterday morning you woke up from your fantasy world. You've been here for over ten years."

Oliver was incredulous. "I have?"

"You have."

"What's wrong with me?"

"You suffer from hallucinatory bipolar disorder; once known as manic depression. It's a mental health condition that causes extreme mood swings—emotional highs and lows. When you hit an extreme low, you lose interest and pleasure in the real world. You also suffer from extremely low self-esteem, mostly related to your inability to find love. You know, a long-term, intimate, and committed relationship. For many years, you've been escaping to the familiar comfort of your dreams. In your dreams, you were finding what you couldn't find in the real world. The one thing every human craves and so few can acquire—true love."

"Oh my God. That's awful."

"Your condition is not completely without hope. With the right treatment, you can lead a relatively normal life."

"But I haven't been up to this point?"

"Well, let's just say our little experiment didn't work the way we'd hoped. Carmen took a shine to you. She started to include you in her little games. Like many people, she also has an unrequited relationship with love and affection. You see, Carmen suffers from hallucinatory multiple personality disorder. She has the ability to construct complex worlds with elaborate characters. These worlds are completely real to her. It's an escape hatch from the real world—a coping mechanism. We reasoned, perhaps erroneously, that your desperate need for a soulmate, along with hers, would bring you both back to reality."

"But that didn't happen?" Oliver said.

Doctor Stevens frowned. "Unfortunately, the opposite happened. You got lured into her world and everything in it became real to you as well. It's really very strange indeed. I've never seen anything like it in my twenty-year professional career as a psychiatrist."

Oliver couldn't believe what he was hearing. "So Sarah, Giselle, and Mark aren't real?"

"They're real all right. At least they were. They've been dead for over five years."

"Holy shit," Oliver said, wiping a sweaty brow and gripping the arms of the chair. "How did they die?"

"They died in a house fire. Carmen and the dolls were the only ones who survived."

"How did the fire start?"

"We believe it was some kind of an accident."

Carmen couldn't kill anybody. Not on purpose anyway. "That's good to know."

"Yes, we're trying to get Carmen to remember, but, unfortunately, she can't yet."

Something else occurred to Oliver. If he'd been here for over ten years, how did he wind up here? Did his parents really die of tragic illnesses when he was just a toddler? Or did he kill them?

And he had to know. "What happened to my parents?"

"Our records show that your parents died of drug-resistant tuberculosis when you were three years old."

"Thank God," Oliver said. "I mean...I mean, I didn't mean it that way."

"I know how you meant it," Doctor Stevens said. "You're relieved you didn't kill them. Right?"

"You're right. Then how did I wind up here?"

"You developed your bipolar disorder many years ago. It was probably triggered by your low self-esteem. You were able to live with it for about a year, but then it worsened and paranoia started to manifest itself. Eventually, you were fired from your customer service job at Bell Canada and sought professional help. We tried many different medications but

your condition worsened and you eventually ended up here—quite voluntarily, I might add."

"You mean I can leave anytime?"

Doctor Stevens pushed his black-framed glasses up the bridge of his nose, magnifying his eyes cartoon-like. "Do you think you're ready to integrate yourself back into society?"

"I guess not," Oliver said, slumping in his chair, defeated, deflated, and depressed all over again. He'd just had his precariously constructed world blown up by a landmine. But Carmen was real. His love for her was real and he was convinced it was mutual. The only thing he wanted to do was hug her tightly, console her with compassionate and tender words, and make all of their problems disappear again. She'd shown him love and affection like never before, and he wanted it back again.

"You're not ready for the real world yet," Doctor Stevens said. "I think we need to work with each of you separately for some time and closely monitor your progress."

Oliver's hopes faded. "You mean I can't see Carmen?"

"I don't think it's a good idea, at least not right now. Maybe never. The risk is too high that you'd both escape into your meticulously constructed dream world and we'd never be able to bring you back. Do you realize that, while we were playing along with your fantasy, the two of you escaped from the institute on more than one occasion?"

Oliver shook his head. "I was in another world at the time."

The doctor stood, signaling the end of the meeting. "I think you've had enough for one day. I know this has hit you like a bombshell and you're gonna need some time to process it. Don't worry, you still have your ward privileges. But Carmen has been transferred to another ward and you won't be able to find her in her room anymore. And you'll have to promise me you won't go snooping around and trying to stir up trouble?"

Oliver slowly rose. "I won't. I promise."

Doctor Stevens slid his glasses down the bridge of his nose, bent his head, and eyed Oliver. "Are you sure? You don't want your ward privileges revoked. You don't want to end up in isolation."

"Cross my heart," Oliver said, drawing an X with his index finger across his chest.

Chapter Twenty-Eight

Six months later. Summer was over. It was the middle of winter. Oliver sat at a desk positioned in front of a window and watched the snow gently blanket the expansive grounds below. Normally, he wasn't a winter guy. Normally, the cold white stuff made him depressed. But not today. That afternoon, it looked so pure, so clean, and so glorious.

The reason? He was filled with nervous excitement and anticipation.

After recovering somewhat from the traumatic shock of the ordeal, Oliver had bided his time obediently, making all the right moves at all the right times. He'd befriended his neighbor across the hall, Harvey Spiller, a paranoid schizophrenic. As it turned out, Harvey had an axe to grind with Doctor Stevens over his unconventional treatment methods. Every day, Oliver would leak a little more information to Harvey about "the experiment" and it didn't take long for Harvey to become infuriated. Somehow, somewhere, someone in a position of authority had gotten wind of Doctor Stevens' unorthodox treatment methods and he'd quietly transferred out of Mississauga Psychiatric Institute, relocating clear across the country to a psychiatric facility in the city of Vancouver. He'd been replaced by a by-the-book doctor called Marvin Standler, who had not taken kindly to the use of patients as laboratory animals and had made it his mission to integrate patients as much as possible. The first thing Standler did was close down the isolation wing where Carmen had been kept.

Oliver had played his cards right. And he'd learned through Harvey, an encyclopedia of hospital gossip and information, that Carmen had played her cards right. In one hour from now, she would be returning to the ward, returning to her old room three doors down the hall from Oliver.

And Oliver believed he was in fine shape to be reunited with the love of his life. He'd played some games with his new anti-depressant medication, fooling the staff into thinking that he'd been taking them. But he'd been pocketing them and the only pills he was taking were the powerful sleeping pills they administered at night. They knocked him out cold and kept the wolves outside the door, particularly Stella, that evil she-wolf.

Glimpses of what Oliver's life used to be had resurfaced. His addiction to the boob tube and junk food, coping mechanisms for the loneliness, sadness, and despair he felt because of his inability to find a female companion. The resulting loss of interest in his personal hygiene and household chores. And finally the terrorizing descent into the black pit of depression, which only led to more junk food, more binge-watching, more neglect of his personal hygiene, and finally resulting in his firing from Bell Canada. How Carmen managed to wipe it all away and bring him along on her meticulously constructed fantasy world he never completely understood and probably never would. But months ago, he'd given up trying. That didn't matter anymore. The only thing that did matter was Carmen would be reunited with him soon and he had concocted a plan that would see them together and happy for the rest of their lives.

He called it Operation Happily-Ever-After.

He sighed. Some things in life would always remain mysteries. Like it or not, that's just the way it was.

Oliver heard a knock on the door and spun around, thinking he'd lost track of time and Carmen had arrived.

"Come in," he said as butterflies began dancing in his stomach.

The door opened part way and Harvey stuck his head inside. He was a tall and wiry man with an unkempt mop of sandy brown hair and piercing green eyes.

"I've got them," Harvey said. "You coming?"

Oliver had almost forgotten. He and Harvey had made a plan to rescue Carmen's dolls from their captivity and return them to her room prior to her arrival.

"Of course," Oliver said, approaching the door. He pulled it all the way open and saw that Harvey held a blue translucent garbage bag containing the three dolls. "Where did you find them?"

"They were in a utility storage room two floors up," Harvey said. "Doctor Standler got Nurse Ramsey to open it up when I explained to him that I had to find Carmen's dolls before she returned to her room otherwise she might have another nervous breakdown. He made me promise to return them to her room, but that part was easy."

"Great work," Oliver said.

Examining the dolls through the see-through plastic, Oliver realized that was another thing he would perhaps never completely understand. He knew Carmen's mother had used them to ward off evil but otherwise knew little about the origin of the magic dolls.

"Do you want one?" Harvey asked. "I thought you said Milton was your doll and you needed him to keep Stella away."

"That was then, this is now. Stella's been killed off, remember? Selina kicked the shit out of her."

"Right," Harvey said, scratching the chin stubble on his sunken face. "I get mixed up sometimes."

"No problem. Let's get going."

Oliver took the lead and Harvey followed. They arrived at 606, Carmen's room, and walked right in the open door. The blinds had been pulled open and bright sunlight painted the room in a soft and warm yellow glow. Someone had thoughtfully placed a dozen red roses on a bedside table. There was a simple white dresser in the room, a freshly made bed, two nightstands, and two chairs, each positioned bedside.

"Where should we put them?" Harvey asked, setting the garbage bag down.

Oliver kneeled down and carefully removed the dolls one by one.

"Here," he said, handing Isabella to Harvey. "Put Isabella on the bedside table and I'll put Milton and Grace on the dresser here."

Harvey did as he was told and then checked his watch. "I better go. She'll be here in like five minutes. I don't wanna interfere with the reunion of two lovebirds."

"Thanks for your help," Oliver said.

Harvey grinned. "Anytime. I can see the dolls are happy to be back."

Oliver studied them. They were all smiling warmly. "It looks like it."

"Oh, I know it for sure. They just thanked me."

"They did?"

"Oh yeah. And those aren't voices in my head. I can tell the difference. Good luck."

Before Oliver could respond, Harvey turned and left.

***

Oliver had acted with decency, politeness, and social distancing when he first saw Carmen enter the room. But as soon as Nurse Ramsey had left, he rushed to the door, closed it quickly, and leaped into Carmen's arms, wrapping her in a warm and tight embrace, kissing her passionately all over her face.

He released her, wiped a few tears from his eyes, and watched her do the same. "I can't believe it. We're finally together."

She sat down on the bed and he joined her.

"I know," she said, her face glowing with glee. "It a miracle."

"How have you been?" he asked.

"I've had my ups and downs, but I'm better now. There is some good news, you know. I've never seen Selina again. Never seen that evil Stella either. Have you?"

"No."

Carmen noticed Isabella, and then the other two dolls. "Oh my God. The dolls. Did you bring them?"

Oliver winked. "With a little help from my friend."

Carmen picked up Isabella, brushed back an errant lock of hair, and kissed her on the cheek. Then she hugged her tightly for a moment before placing her back on the nightstand.

"Thank you," she said. "They look happy to be back."

"They do," Oliver agreed. "Harvey said they thanked him."

A crease furrowed Carmen's brow. "Who's Harvey?"

"The friend who helped get them back."

"You've had time to make friends... while I've been in isolation. Have you been okay?"

Oliver nodded slowly. "I've been biding my time until I could see you again. In the meantime, I hatched a plan to get rid of Stevens."

"I heard."

"You did?"

"Yeah. Nurse Ramsey told me he's been transferred."

"With Harvey's help, I spread the word about his unconventional methods. Once they transferred him, the first thing Doctor Standler did was shut down the isolation wing."

"So you basically got me outta there," Carmen said.

"With a little help from a friend."

"Thank you."

"I had to do it. I missed you so much."

"Me too," Carmen said, placing a hand on his knee. "What do we do now? I mean, they're not gonna let us, you know, be together like we want to."

"I have a plan."

Carmen's face brightened. Isolation hadn't been particularly kind to her and she had dark circles under her eyes and a few new creases on her forehead. She'd also lost about ten pounds. "You mean we're gonna escape?"

"You want to?"

"Of course," Carmen said. "After the life we had, I couldn't imagine spending the rest of my life in here. Can you?"

"No. We have to find the bliss we had after we destroyed Stella."

"You said you have a plan?"

"I'll tell you all about it tonight, okay? It's called Operation Happily-Ever-After."

"I love it," Carmen said, hugging Oliver tightly. "And guess what?"

"What?" Oliver asked, his eyes beginning to water.

Carmen planted three wet kisses on his cheek. "I love you."

"And I love you... more than you'll ever know."

Chapter Twenty-Nine

Doctor Marvin Standler ran a hand through his neatly cropped grey hair and stared at the bed in stunned silence. His efforts to reform Mississauga Psychiatric Institute and implement more patient integration had been going so well up until this grim incident.

There, not four feet in front of him, were the bodies of Carmen and Oliver, wrapped in a tight embrace, both smiling peacefully.

Both quite dead.

There would be hell to pay, he knew, and he wasn't looking forward to the repercussions. A full investigation and a full review of his methods, potentially resulting in the loss of his career and being black-balled and discredited for the rest of his life. All because that wacko Doctor Stevens had allowed these two mentally ill patients to pursue a fantasy world that had become so powerful and real that it had ultimately led to their untimely deaths. Not to mention Carmen's solitary confinement, not to mention Oliver being used as a laboratory rat to test out multiple types of anti-depressant medications. Perhaps well-intentioned, but in the end, one monumental fuck up. Even if he wanted to, and he wasn't that kind of a doctor, he couldn't cover it up.

Both Carmen and Oliver had pill bottles clenched tightly in their hands. They'd been dead for over eight hours. They'd evidently made a suicide pact last night and had wasted no time executing it.

"Are you okay?" Nurse Ramsey said, touching his arm gently.

"No, I'm not okay," Doctor Standler said evenly. "And pardon my language, but if I go down for this, I'll make damn sure I take that fucking wacko Doctor Stevens with me."

"I... I better call the orderlies to remove the bodies before the other patients wake up," Nurse Ramsey said, backing toward the door.

Doctor Standler wiped tiny droplets of perspiration from his upper lip and glanced around the room. "What happened to the dolls? I thought you said you'd arranged for them to be delivered to Carmen's room?"

"I did. I saw them here yesterday."

"Well, then what happened to them?"

"I have no idea."

Epilogue

Waking up in the richly textured and dark red bedroom of his ancient castle in another world, Oliver felt under the covers and sighed when his hand reached the warm naked flesh of Carmen's thigh. Before moving, he listened intently until he heard her steady breathing. Satisfied, he climbed out of bed, careful not to wake her. There would be time enough for that. After the traumatizing ordeal she'd been through, she needed a few more hours of beauty sleep. And, besides, he had a lot to do right now.

He plucked his burgundy velvet robe from a nearby decorative hanger, put it on, and quietly left the room, closing the door softly behind him. As he busied himself arranging tables and chairs in the ornate ballroom, he reflected on the overwhelming success of Operation Happily-Ever-After.

It might not be to everyone's taste, but it suited Carmen and Oliver just fine. They were finally together, irrevocably together, and with none of the constraints of the material world. They could eat when they pleased, drink when they pleased, and fly around the castle rooms and corridors drunk for all anybody cared. In short, they could do whatever they wanted whenever they wanted. And since arriving here a week ago, all they had wanted to do was make love. All of their pent-up passion had finally been released and they'd spent most of the last week in fervent displays of mutually satisfying lovemaking. After their sexual libidos had been satiated enough for them to think rationally, they'd decided a party was in order.

They'd invited all of their friends—both imaginary and real. Not that Oliver knew the difference anymore, and not that he really cared.

Sliding a large table near the front of the ballroom, he felt a rush of warm air and turned around.

"Up here," Finley said.

Oliver saw both Finley and his wife, Ruby, floating a few feet above him, both draped in angelic white robes. They each held gleaming silver trays that were filled with wine bottles.

"Where do you want these?" Ruby asked.

"Over here," Oliver said, satisfied he had positioned the table exactly where he wanted it. "This table is reserved for the hosts and the guests of honor."

Oliver moved on to more table-and-chair-arranging as Finley and Ruby carefully set the wine on the reserved table. When they were done, they flew off into the kitchen to get more party supplies.

Oliver finished setting the last table and gazed up at the water fountain, right beside the guest-of-honor table. He studied the naked, water-spewing-bow-and-arrow-armed cupid at the top and marveled at the irony. It was once a part of his dreams and once a part of his fantasy world. Now it was his real world. *If people really knew what the afterlife was like, they'd be dying to get in.*

He chuckled and moved on to the vibrantly colored plush sofas and chairs, dusting them meticulously until they looked perfect. They had to be perfect. This celebration, after all, had to be seamless because it was the celebration of a perfect union—a match made in heaven.

"Guess what?" Carmen said, bursting out of the bedroom, her voice echoing musically throughout the ballroom.

Oliver watched as she floated across the room and right into his waiting and wanting arms. She was smiling broadly. She hugged him tightly for a moment before releasing him and soaring around the room in a circle and finally landing beside him on the gleaming floor.

"I had a dream," she said. "I know what happened."

"What do you mean?"

"I know what really happened to my mom and Mark and Giselle."

Carmen had Oliver's full attention. This was something he wanted to hear. "What happened?"

"It was nobody's fault. It was an electrical fire caused by faulty wiring. It started in the basement. I was down there at the time getting vegetables out of the root cellar when I saw the sparks. I tried to warn everyone, but it was too late. It had already engulfed the kitchen by the time I got upstairs."

"That's a relief," Oliver said. "I mean, that you didn't kill them. But I never doubted you for a second. You couldn't kill anybody."

"Don't you see?" Carmen said. "This is a breakthrough. All these years I've been blaming myself. All these years I blocked out what really happened because I felt such overwhelming guilt for not being able to rescue my family."

Oliver floated over to her and held her as tears spilled down her cheeks, splashing onto his robe.

"It's okay now, honey. Everything's gonna be okay."

After a few minutes, Carmen regained some of her composure. Looking around the room, she said, "I see you've been busy."

"It's gonna be a great party," Oliver said. "I've invited almost everyone."

Carmen's eyes darkened. "Not Stella?"

"No, of course not. But Milton, Grace, and Isabella are coming."

Carmen's eyes widened. "You mean I get to meet them for real—in the real world?"

"That's right, honey."

"What about my mother?"

"She's coming."

"Excellent. I can't wait to see her again." Carmen dropped her eyes to the floor. "And Mark and Giselle?"

"I invited them," Oliver said. "They haven't confirmed yet, but I hope they make it. Forgive and forget, right?"

"I suppose you're right."

"And you'll never guess who else is coming?"

After a pause, Carmen said, "It can't be Selina. She's in heaven... or she's in your dreams."

"No," Oliver said. "She's in heaven. Exactly where we are. And my dreams are now my new reality."

Carmen grinned and planted a wet kiss on Oliver's lips. "You're only half right."

"Half right?"

"Yeah. *Our* dreams are now *our* new reality."

Also by William Blackwell

Phantom Rage, Poison Rage, Infected Rage
Nightmare's Edge
Resurrection Point
Brainstorm
Rule 14
Assaulted Souls
Assaulted Souls II
Assaulted Souls III
Blood Curse
Black Dawn
The Strap
The End is Nigh
Orgon Conclusion
Freaky Franky
The Witch's Tombstone
The Dark Menace
Tales of Damnation
In Your Dreams
Macabre Alley
A Head for an Eye

The Dark Menace Preview

"*The Dark Menace* isn't just horror, it's a descent into fear, sleep, and madness. Gripping, emotional, and rooted in chilling reality. If you've ever felt watched in the dark, this story will haunt you. Absolutely compelling." -Jessica Raye

Noah Janzen is plagued by nightmares and numerous sleep disorders; night terrors, sleepwalking, sleep talking, and a terrifying sleep paralysis that often invokes chilling images of the Shadow People and the Hat Man.

Determined to prevent his nocturnal demons from interfering with his successful career and newly formed relationship with Angela Rosewood, he meets her in a local pub. But when he sees a shadowy figure wearing a fedora and a trench coat eerily watching him through a window, he freaks out and flees.

He soon learns that a hat-wearing psycho has viciously attacked Angela, smashing in her door, trashing her apartment, and nearly killing her. Worse still, Angela suspects Noah has morphed into a conduit for evil and starts distancing herself from him. She might even think he is the Hat Man.

Desperate to save his new relationship and find answers, he seeks the aid of physicist and sleep specialist, Doctor Neil Samuelson. While remaining tight-lipped on his experiments involving the Shadow People and the Hat Man, the enigmatic doctor informs Noah that an old woman has been brutally murdered at the hands of *The Dark Menace*.

As blood-curdling reports of Shadow People and the Hat Man escalate, Noah suspects Neil has accidentally opened up a portal from another dimension, unleashing a torrent of shadowy evil entities, hell-bent on terrorizing and destroying humanity.

He's thrust into an epic battle to preserve his relationship and sanity and find answers to a strange and mysterious real-life phenomenon that has haunted and terrorized thousands of people around the world for centuries.

About the Author

Canadian dark fiction author William Blackwell studied journalism at Mount Royal University and English literature at The University of British Columbia. He worked as a journalist for many years before pursuing his passion for storytelling. His novels have been characterized as graphic, edgy, and at times terrifying. Currently living on a secluded acreage on Prince Edward Island, Blackwell finds much of his inspiration from Mother Nature, odd people, traveling, and bizarre nightmares.

Author Comments

Thank you for reading this book. I would be eternally grateful if you would post a book review on your favorite book retailer website. A positive review is the highest compliment a writer can receive. Reviews are crucial to the success of any author and also help readers discover new books. You don't have to say much. A few sentences will suffice.

In other news, I have a gift for you. Complete the signup form in the link below with your name and email address and download a FREE copy of *Resurrection Point*, a dark tale about the horrifying consequences of experimenting with death and resurrection. You're only agreeing to be kept up to date on blog posts, new releases, and freebies. I promise I won't spam you and you can unsubscribe at any time.

Thanks again for your support.

http://www.wblackwell.com/free-ebook/

www.ingramcontent.com/pod-product-compliance
Lightning Source LLC
Chambersburg PA
CBHW030302200626
46816CB00002BA/736